Joseph Fitzgerald Molloy

The Romance of the Irish Stage

Vol. 1

Joseph Fitzgerald Molloy

The Romance of the Irish Stage
Vol. 1

ISBN/EAN: 9783337348311

Printed in Europe, USA, Canada, Australia, Japan

Cover: Foto ©Andreas Hilbeck / pixelio.de

More available books at **www.hansebooks.com**

THE ROMANCE

OF

THE IRISH STAGE

WITH PICTURES OF THE IRISH CAPITAL IN THE EIGHTEENTH CENTURY

BY

J. FITZGERALD MOLLOY

VOL. I.

NEW YORK

DODD, MEAD AND COMPANY

1897

PREFACE.

THE Romance of the Irish Stage lies in the histories of those who have fretted their hours upon its boards.

During the Eighteenth Century no other country could boast of so many notable players; in themselves adventurous and fascinating personages, admirably fitted by a national temperament for the art in which they excelled. Fiction might borrow from fact such swift and daring transitions, such amazing episodes as these that enliven their careers.

Charles Macklin, abandoning his more Hibernian name and his saddler's trade to gain fair renown as a comedian and playwright; Tom Sheridan, flying in the face of family pride and hostile prejudice, and casting aside his college cap and gown to don sock and buskin; Peg Woffington, orange seller and booth dancer, gaining place as the first actress

v

of her day; Spranger Barry, quitting his silversmith's shop to become the idol of Smock
Alley Theatre; the beautiful Miss Bellamy,
daughter of an Irish peer and heroine of a
hundred intrigues, arrested by bailiffs in her
gilded sedan chair; Henry Mossop, rival of
Garrick and dupe of a gambling courtess,
dying heart-broken in a garret; Dorothy
Jordan, the milliner's apprentice, capturing at
first essay the admiration of the town ; Richard
Daly, the young gentleman out of Galway who
fought sixteen duels in three years, and lived
to introduce Mrs. Siddons to an Irish audience
—all are children of the Celt, the incidents of
whose lives clothe themselves in the witching
raiment of romance.

In this, as in his former works, the writer
has placed the records of the town beside the
history of the stage, one being a reflection of
the other, a study of each seeming necessary to
the understanding of both. And as a picture
of social life in the Irish capital during the
Eighteenth Century has not heretofore been
painted, it is hoped this presentment may
please; for no more splendid and varied

panorama can be imagined than Dublin in its pre-Union days, with its state processions, its parliament, its court festivities, its reckless gambling, duelling, and abductions, its roystering and extravagance, the whole illumined by a gaiety that has become a tradition.

In striving to present the period with vividness, innumerable histories, biographies, newssheets, playbills, and manuscripts have been consulted. As a hundred exposures of a camera may be necessary to the production of a single animated photograph, so a score or more volumes, at an average, have contributed to the writing of a chapter. A whole library may be said to be condensed in this book, covering a century and describing events connected with the stage and the town.

J. FITZGERALD MOLLOY.

CONTENTS.

ix

CONTENTS

CHAPTER IV.

CHAPTER V.

CHAPTER VI.

CHAPTER VII.

CONTENTS

CHAPTER VIII.

CHAPTER IX.

CHAPTER X.

THE

ROMANCE OF THE IRISH STAGE.

CHAPTER I.

Accident to Smock Alley Theatre — The ambition of
Thomas Elrington, manager — Laying hold of a
ghost — Madame Violante comes to town — The
entertainments of a booth—The English Gladiator—
Managers three—Lord Mountcashel's noble example
—New theatres arise—Lacy Ryan and Denny Delane
— Keeping a birthday — The opening of Aungier
Street Theatre.

THERE was no doubt that an accident had happened, though a tragedy had been averted. As
the occurrence took place late on the night of
the 26th of December, 1701, the news had not
spread over the city of Dublin until the following morning, when vast crowds, neglectful of
such unexciting matters as their own business,
assembled round the entrance of Smock Alley
Theatre to see for themselves that the galleries
had fallen, and to discourse of such details as
might be forthcoming.

To a people emotional and dramatic, picturesque, eloquent, vivid, and imaginative by
temperament, the theatre was a centre of
attraction, an object of interest, a familiar and
delightful place whose fortunes concerned them,
whose productions occupied them, whose
players were as familiar friends. The stage
was not less to them than it had been to the
Greeks of an earlier day; that gracious race
whose spirit they shared if not inherited.

Therefore, in the raw cold morn of the dying
year, whilst mists rising from the adjacent Liffey
hung in the atmosphere, this throng of fine
gentlemen and worthy citizens, tradesmen and
mechanics, hackney coachmen, chair-men, and
apprentices, oyster wenches, orange sellers,
ballad singers, and beggars by profession,
gathered together, talking in chorus and ges-
ticulating, stirred to greater animation and
closer intimacy by sight of what they considered
a common loss.

And there was the playhouse itself, its interior
to which free entrance was permitted, brooded
over by semi-darkness which the ruddy glare
of a few torches did little to dispel; a pro-

digious pile of rubbish indicating the fallen galleries, dust lying thick on the damask seats close to the stage, cushions torn, springs exposed, twisted iron and torn backs of benches protruding in unexpected places; a sorry sight in all, which it was rumoured the Lord Lieutenant himself was coming in his coach to witness.

By the surging crowd, struggling for a better sight of the disaster, its cause was forgotten for awhile; but soon rumours most strange were afloat that lent a supernatural air to what otherwise might have seemed a commonplace occurrence, and to the minds of many settled the matter to their entire satisfaction. Such ordinary considerations as weak supports and undue crowding of the galleries were scouted; sure, all good Christians knew the destruction of the house was due to a performance of Shadwell's Libertine, a loose play wholly unsuited for representation.

That the accident was merited, was readily admitted by those who had been unable to obtain entrance the previous evening; and there were many in the crowd who declared "that during the comedy the candles burnt blue and went out; that two or three times a dancer extraordinary whom nobody knew was seen, and that he had a cloven foot": a fact that made his personality suspected.

In due time the galleries were re-erected and the doors of Smock Alley playhouse were opened to the public, who were gratified by the performance of tragedies and comedies they had seen scores of times and knew by heart as well as the players themselves; but Shadwell's "Libertine" was placed upon the shelf and not played again in this house for upwards of twenty years.

The manager of the theatre at the time of this occurrence was Joseph Ashbury, a Londoner by birth, who, in genteel parlance, had received "a classic education at Eton School" and had come into Ireland with the Duke of Ormond, then Lord Lieutenant, who had made him one of the gentlemen of his retinue and subsequently Master of the Revels. Having got together a fair company, most of them hired in London, Ashbury began his management of Smock Alley Theatre in

March, 1692, when the tragedy of Othello was performed with vast credit and profit to the players and to the great satisfaction of the town.

Joseph Ashbury, who continued for many years to direct the fortunes of Smock Alley Theatre, was a player of much excellence, and moreover was considered the best teacher of elocution in the three kingdoms. Chetwood describes him as being a person of an advantageous height, with a "countenance that demanded a reverential awe, a full, meaning eye, and a sweet-sounding, manly voice." In his day he held the proud position of Master of the Revels in Ireland under Charles II., James II., William III., Queen Anne, and George I.

Having done much to place the drama on a sound footing in the Irish capital, he died on the 24th of July, 1720, and was succeeded as manager by his son-in-law, Thomas Elrington, under whose reign we are enabled to catch a closer view of the Irish stage and its performers. A member of a large family, Thomas Elrington was born in London, and early in his days had been apprenticed to a French upholsterer in Covent Garden. Distaste for his work and love of the theatre were equally strong in him, and such leisure as he had was given to the reading of plays, and later to the performance of parts in the private theatres which at that date were common to the locality mentioned. The French upholsterer, being a good tradesman and a harsh master, discouraged by word and deed the leanings of his apprentice.

It happened one evening that whilst this lank youth was playing the ghost in Hamlet in a full suit of pasteboard armour, the fat little Frenchman found his way into the theatre, much to the poor ghost's consternation. And when in a quavering voice more fitted to the fear of those who beheld him than to one who dwelt no longer among men, the troubled spirit said " Mark me," the unimpressed and wrathful upholsterer replied aloud " Me vil mark you presently," and without more ado he got on the stage and laid heavy hands on the ghost, who rushed out of the house and through the streets, strokes sounding loud on the paste-board armour, the audience joining in the chase with the intention of rescuing the ghost from such unhandsome treatment, and bringing him back to harrow their souls: in which good purpose they finally succeeded.

It seemed evident now that Elrington's inclinations pledged him to the stage beyond recall; for soon after he was engaged to play at Drury Lane at ten shillings a week, the salary then commonly given to young actors and gratefully received by them. From London he crossed to Dublin, being hired by Ashbury for Smock Alley, whose patrons he greatly pleased. Here he acted characters of consequence with much reputation to himself; and indeed, whether he was seen in tragedy or comedy, he was reckoned by judges one of the best actors of his time. We are assured that his voice and person could scarce be equalled — the one being shapely, the other sweet — and his manners were highly engaging. One of his ardent admirers used to mention as a striking merit in Elrington, that whilst on the stage he could be heard all over the neighbouring quay, whilst the voices of other performers could scarce be caught beyond the theatre walls.

To such good purpose did he play his part in private life, that within twelve months of his arrival he gained the hand of his manager's daughter, with whom he lived happily for many a day. Fortune favoured him in various ways besides those narrated already; for not only did he succeed his father-in-law as manager of Smock Alley Theatre, but likewise as Master of the Revels and Steward to the King's Inns of Court. Moreover, a post in the Quit Rent Office was given him, and he was made a gunner in the train of Artillery, a gift of his friend Lord Mountjoy. His popularity with a hospitable and appreciative people was great. On one occasion when, after passing some months in London, he returned to Dublin, bells were rung, bonfires lighted, and there was great rejoicing in the houses of many citizens to welcome him. Indeed, it was the truthful boast of this much honoured actor that there was not "a gentleman's house in the kingdom of Ireland to which he was not a welcome visitant."

Whilst Smock Alley Theatre was entertaining its patrons with such plays as Cato; King Richard the Third, "a tragedy written by the famous

Shakespeare;" Alexander the Great; The Comical Revenge, or Love in a Tub; The Man of Mode, and the comedies of the witty George Farquhar, a student of Trinity College, a French lady named Madame Violante came to town in 1727, and without further ado hired a fine residence in Fownes Court that had once been occupied by the Lord Chancellor Whitchel. This house was not only uncommonly roomy, but possessed a spacious yard which was converted into a booth where a first-class company of rope-dancers, swordsmen, and tumblers exhibited themselves to the delight of the town for some time. The lady herself, though no longer young, and never beautiful, tripped about her stage in an amazing way. Chetwood was informed that her " showing her limbs did not meet with the success in this kingdom as she had found " in England; a sad reproof to a gallant nation.

One of her company, Mr. Figg, " the English gladiator," secured more popularity, and confided to the historian of the stage just mentioned, as an instance of his success, that he had not bought a shirt for more than twenty years, but had sold some dozens within that time.

"It was his method," writes Chetwood, "when he fought in his Amphitheatre (his stage having that superb title), to send round to a select number of his scholars to borrow a shirt for the ensuing combat, and seldom failed of half a dozen of superfine Holland from his prime pupils (most of the young nobility and gentry made it part of their education to march under his warlike banner). This champion was generally conqueror, though his shirt seldom failed of gaining a cut from his enemy, and sometimes his flesh, though I think he never received any dangerous wound. Most of his scholars were at every battle, and were sure to exult at their great master's victories, every person supposing he saw the wounds his shirt received. Mr. Figg took his opportunity to inform his lenders of linen of the chasms their shirts received, with a promise to send them home. But, said the ingenious, courageous Figg, I seldom received any other answer than ' Damn you, keep it.' "

After a while the rope-dancing, sparring, and tumbling had ceased to draw the town, when the energetic Madame Violante converted her booth into a playhouse for the performance of

farce. The company she engaged were poor
creatures at best, and so failed to attract, when
the manageress bethought her of producing the
Beggar's Opera, then held in high esteem,
with children for players. The novelty of the
sight, the ability of the actors, and the merits
of the piece, combined to attract full houses,
and nothing was spoken of but Miss Betty
Barnes as Captain Macheath; and Master
Sparks as Peachum; and Master Beamfly
as Locket; but above and beyond all, Peg
Woffington as Polly gained universal applause.
For here it was that the child who afterwards
became the greatest actress of her day first
made an appearance that gave ample promise
of a talent subsequently perfected.

For four years Madame Violante continued
to entertain in Fownes Court, but in 1731 she
removed to more commodious premises in
George's Lane, the former booth being rented by
some players of considerable merit who, having
revolted from the Smock Alley Theatre, went
into management for themselves.

Their hopes of success were quickly un-
deceived; for soon they were obliged to close

their doors, and their opposition, whilst injuring themselves, did little harm to Smock Alley Theatre. Nor did the new music-hall in Crow Street, which opened with a ridotto on November 30th, 1731, much interfere with the fortunes of the principal playhouse, which continued to prosper until the death of its manager on the 22nd of July, 1732.

Three months later Smock Alley Theatre opened once more under the triple management of Francis Elrington, brother of the late patentee, Lewis Layfield, once a member of the Drury Lane Company, and Thomas Griffith, an Irishman by birth, a mathematical instrument maker by training, and an actor by choice. Great preparations preceded the event; the house had been cleaned, repaired, and beautified; new scenes were ordered, and new machinery imported for the production of The Island Princess, an opera with which the season opened. To further encourage the managers, my Lord Mountcashel, as may be learned from *Faulkner's Journal*, " gave them a present of five suits of the finest laced and embroidered cloaths that ever were seen on any stage; " and a little later the same paper states, " The fine cloaths lately given by the Right Hon. Lord Mountcashel were for the use of the whole company, and it is hoped our nobility and gentry will follow that noble and generous example."

For a while all went well, but soon the management met with an opposition which seriously alarmed them. It appears that Madame Violante, finding her business decline, let her theatre to three young and ambitious players, Luke Sparks, John Barrington, and Miss Mackay, for three pounds a week, " No great sum, but as much as they were able to pay." The worthy trio were joined by others who hoped to win fame and gain profit by the stage. Though they had neither new clothes nor scenery, and their costumes were of the poorest, they were not disheartened. The audaciousness of youth supporting them, they set out by playing Farquhar's comedies, and several people of quality interesting themselves in their adventure the town flocked to see them.

So long as tumblers, fencers, dancers, and children had filled this stage, it was not considered as a rival by the managers of Smock Alley Theatre; but now it was occupied by a regular company, their resentment rose, and laying their case before the Lord Mayor, they besought his Worship to interpose his authority and forbid all performances at Fownes Court. With this request the worthy man readily complied, and the little theatre was closed, much to the indignation of the town. Indeed, so warmly was the matter taken up, and so great was the indignation felt, that subscriptions were speedily forthcoming to build a playhouse outside the jurisdiction of the Lord Mayor, where he could exercise no authority.

The site selected for the new building was Rainsford Street, a considerable distance from the centre of the town, and within the liberty of the Earl of Meath, who granted a licence for its erection to Thomas Walker at a rent of forty pounds a year; the said sum to be distributed amongst the poor. The theatre was strongly built and capable of accommodating a hundred pounds at common prices. The company who had been turned out of Fownes Court sought their fortunes in the new house, which was opened towards the end of 1732.

There were now two regular theatres in Dublin, and a third was soon to be built. Four years before Thomas Elrington's death, rumours regarding the unsafe condition of Smock Alley house spread abroad, when to silence so injurious a report the manager had it examined by Thomas Burgh, engineer and surveyor-general, who publicly certified that " the theatre was safe, and would bear any number of people who should please to resort thither."

In 1732, as already stated, it had been repaired, but soon it became evident that no amount of patching would save it from decay, and it was therefore resolved to build a new playhouse. The scheme being laid before the public, a great number of " men of the first rank and most distinguished understandings " subscribed for its erection with spirit and promptitude, " they being convinced of the great utility a theatre properly conducted may prove to a rising nation."

A site of ground adjoining Aungier Street,

the fashionable end of the town, was secured, and the first stone of the new theatre was laid by the Right Hon. Richard Tighe, the second by the Hon. General Napier, the third by William Tighe, and the fourth by the Hon. Sir Edward Loveit Pearce, Surveyor-General to His Majesty's Works in Ireland and architect of the Parliament House. Medals struck for the occasion were placed under each stone by Elrington, Griffith, and Layfield, managers of Smock Alley. The date of this ceremony was the 8th of May, 1733, a day which was regarded by the people as a general holiday. From an early hour in the morning a prodigious concourse of people had gathered in the neighbouring streets, which were decorated with flags and hung with bunting and festoons of evergreens. Each stone of the building was laid with a flourish of trumpets, drums, a band of music, and the loud acclamations of the public. " Plenty of the choicest wines were provided for the gentry by the managers; several barrels of ale were given to the populace; each of the gentlemen who laid the foundation stones made presents to the workmen; after which

16

an elegant dinner was provided by the managers for the nobility and gentry," as Robert Hitchcock records.

Whilst the new theatre was being built, performances were given as usual at the old, and the regular company was strengthened by the addition of Lacy Ryan and Denny Delane, useful members of the Drury Lane company, and prime favourites with the public in Ireland and England.

Lacy Ryan was Irish by descent but a Londoner by birth, and a pupil of St. Paul's School. He was originally destined for the law, and bound to an attorney, but the glamour of the stage falling on him, he resolved to become a player, and had the good fortune to be introduced by Sir Richard Steele to the manager of the Haymarket Theatre. By the latter he was given small parts to play, amongst them being Seyton, an officer in Macbeth, which he, being then sixteen years, played in a full-bottomed wig. Two years later he won the admiration of the town by his representation of Marcus, in Cato, for which he had been selected by its author, and from that time he rose to a conspicuous place in his profession.

But it was not alone on the stage that he gained notoriety, for it happened one night whilst supping at the Sun tavern, in Long Acre, that he with others was beset by one Kelly, a drunkard, a braggart, and a bully, who had long been the dread of all peace-loving people. Ryan protested, whereon Kelly drew his sword and made three thrusts at him before the player could reach his weapon, which he had placed in the window. But no sooner did he gain his sword than Ryan made good use of it by running Kelly through the breast and ridding the public of a scoundrel. So favourably was the act considered, that he was not even obliged to stand his trial for the same.

Fate would have it that he was to suffer from weapons, for some years later when he was returning home late at night through Covent Garden, he was stopped by a footpad. Ryan resisted, when the scurvy fellow up with his pistol and put a bullet through the actor's mouth. And no sooner was this done, than by the light of a lamp to which they had moved somewhat closer, the robber recognized his man, on which he heartily begged pardon, and made away without taking any money. Ryan's face was injured, and what was worse, his voice sounded unpleasant " till the discordance of it became familiar to the ear."

The town was much disturbed by this occurrence to a favourite, and not only did it suffer without murmur the shrillness of his voice, but the nobility and gentry made him handsome presents, and expressed great sympathy for his misfortune.

Denny Delane was the descendant of an ancient Irish family, and had received a college education in old Trinity. Whilst a student he became stage-struck, and at the terrible risk of disgracing himself and all belonging to him, who had never soiled their hands by earning a penny piece, he made bold to apply to Elrington for an engagement. As he had an elegant figure entirely, a voice that would charm the birds off the bushes, and added to that, was mighty handsome, sure enough he obtained what he asked.

Never was such a lover seen on the stage; ladies of quality smiled on him sweetly from the recesses of their boxes, their hearts were his assuredly; and as for the deities sitting in judgment aloft in a semi-obscurity that lent mystery to their personalities, young Denny Delane was their darling. But when in 1731 he was offered extraordinary high terms by Gifford, of Goodman's Fields, London, the gay deceiver left his country and his admirers behind him for the sake of the Saxon's gold. From Goodman's Fields Theatre he went to Drury Lane, the sphere of his success proving wider with his years; but in the summer season he sometimes returned to dear old Dublin, where he was sure to be welcomed with open arms and honeyed words.

Delane and Ryan drew fine houses and gave great satisfaction, and at the end of July they, with the other members of Smock Alley Theatre, set off for the provinces. The town now began to clear, the citizens betaking themselves to the seaside, down to Dalkey, with its yellow beach, and Killiney, with its green hills, and to the villages of Bray and Kingstown, for the remainder of the summer.

It was not until November 24th, 1733, that Smock Alley Theatre once more opened its doors, when the season began by what was then known as a Government play, from the fact that the manager received an annual sum from the Government for the performance of plays on certain nights, such as the birthdays of the King and Queen, and the anniversary of King William's accession.

His Majesty's birthday, November 4th, was regarded as a special feast by a large number of the public, and the doings which occupied them on such occasions will best illustrate the spirit of the age. In the *Dublin Daily Advertiser* we read that, "Amongst other testimonies of the loyalty of the city, the gentlemen of the Ratteen Club, each man dressed in ratteen with an orange-coloured cockade in his hat, went out early in the morning to the hills of Saggord, where in honour of the day they hunted with Sir Compton Dornville's hounds, and after some hours of fine diversion they went to Temple Oge, where they spent the evening in

loyal healths and in commemoration of the
hero of the day."

It was the custom on this date for the Lord
Lieutenant to receive in the morning at the
Castle all loyal subjects amongst the nobility
and gentry who "paid the compliments usual
to such occasions." Then the Lord Mayor and
his sheriffs entertained the Viceroy and a
great number of distinguished people at a
banquet, the finest imaginable, at which long
speeches were made and deep toasts were
drunk and vast quantities eaten.

After this the gallant company got into their
coaches and carriages as best they could, and
were driven to the theatre, where his Excellency
"entertained the nobility and gentry with a
play," which awaited his appearance to begin.
He was received at the door by the managers
carrying wax lights, which must have seemed
extraordinarily numerous to his eyes as he was
conducted to his box. The house invariably
presented a most splendid appearance on those
nights, the ladies being "always complimented
with the freedom of the boxes, and none but

those of the first rank and distinction ever availing themselves of the privilege."

On such a night, on November 4th, 1712, an event occurred which caused great commotion. Rowe's play Tamerlane, a tragedy much in favour with the Whigs, was bespoken. The Lords Justices, who happened to be Tories, forbade the recitation of the prologue, which even more than the play was supposed to contain political allusions. On this occasion, when the prologue had been demanded by a certain portion of the house, and been refused by the manager, a lively youth named Dudley Moor, brother to my Lord Tullamore, leaped upon the stage and boldly recited the lines believed to be "a handsome encomium of King William." Next day the manager, with three others, swore information against Dudley Moor and his associates, who were bound to appear at the Queen's Bench. However, their trial never took place. Two years later, Dudley Moor, whilst in London, spilt his hot blood in a duel which arose from his violent partisanship of the House of Hanover, and proved fatal to him; for in such poor causes may men lose their lives.

Meanwhile the Aungier Street Theatre was being rapidly built, so that on Saturday evening, May 19th, 1734, it was thrown open to the public, whose expectations concerning it had been raised to an uncommon height. The play selected for the occasion was Farquhar's ever popular Recruiting Officer, and the Lord Lieutenant, his Grace the Duke of Dorset, who delighted in witnessing plays, in talking to players, and in patronizing all the diversions of the day — a quality which greatly endeared him to the people he governed — promised to be present.

The Duke proved as good as his word and came with his Duchess, a company of dragoons that made the pavements ring and the mud splash, following their coach with its six horses, its outriders, its velvet-clad footmen with their wands. And behind them came a string of carriages that emptied the Castle of its guests, its suite of attendants, and its officers. When the galleries, which had been crowded for hours, caught sight of their Graces, a hearty welcoming cheer greeted them, that drowned the sound of the orchestra, strumming its loyal ditty. Then under the soft yet dazzling light of wax candles in their brass sconces, what a sight was to be seen? Fair women with patches on cheek and feathers on head, and diamonds galore upon their white necks; and brave men in fine-laced coats of all colours in the rainbow; stars and ribbons on many a swelling breast, and wigs on every head. What a waving of fans and rattling of swords, and interchange of bows and courtesies, before they settled down to hear Griffith speak the prologue, which though not well heard was received with applause; and with what laughter they greeted the witticisms of the play they had witnessed so often already, but which they enjoyed none the less.

Youth and rank and beauty, the sparkle of jewels, the exhilarating blending of rich colours, the rustle of silks and satins, the sound of soft voices, an atmosphere of pleasure, were there, and the night promised well for the fortunes of the new playhouse.

CHAPTER II.

To understand the position it held, and to appreciate the influence it exercised, it would be well to regard the Irish stage in the eighteenth century as the central object in a picture of the Irish capital at the same period.

At a time when the joyousness of existence was unstifled by the hardships of poverty; when life was a thing to love and hold light; when abductions and duels were daily occurrences; when romance and adventure stirred the hearts of a wayward and impressionable people—the streets of their capital reflected their character, as will a room the temperament of its occupant.

And few, if any, were the cities in Europe whose thoroughfares exhibited such brightness and bustle as did those of Dublin. Their centres were blocked from midday till three of the clock, the fashionable dinner hour; and from eight in the evening, the time for routs and assemblies, until early in the morning, by the chairs of women of quality who seldom walked abroad—convenient and, in days of ease and leisure, delightful conveyances, gold-mounted, lined with brocade, and emblazoned with armorial bearings; whilst coaches big as state beds, with outriders, coachmen and footmen in gorgeous liveries, drove their occupants to the Castle levées, the balls given by the nobility, or to the Parliament House, where sat two hundred and forty-nine temporal and twenty-two spiritual peers, with three hundred commoners.

And all day long, and far into the night, there flocked backwards and forwards, through wide streets and narrow, crowds that to modern eyes would seem strangely picturesque—so quaint were their costumes, so varied in colour, so distinctive of class and calling. For here was the sober citizen in his dark blue or plum-coloured suit of broadcloth, with long flaps to his waistcoat, worsted stockings rolled at the knee, and full periwig; the physician in solemn black, with lace ruffles ; military men of all grades who invariably wore their uniforms; the dandy in his green or blue cabinet coat with silver or gold brandenburgs ; the lawyers in great wigs and long cravats ; the running footmen who carried letters and messages, dressed in white jackets and coloured sashes, black velvet caps, staffs in their hands some seven feet high surmounted by the crests of their masters; the university student in his gown.

And in their midst might be seen such well-known and noted figures as my Lord Trimles-town, dressed in scarlet with a full-powdered wig, a diamond brooch in his ruffles, an agate snuff-box in his hands ; and Lord Taffee, tall and thin, in a whole suit of dove-coloured silk ; and Lord Gormanston, who would wear nothing but blue ; and Lord Clanricarde, in full regi-mentals, who, whenever he went abroad, called for his pistols as regularly as for his gloves ; and Lord Howth who not only adopted the

wig with its little rows of curls, and the drab-
coloured coat of a coachman, but likewise his
manners and phraseology, it pleasing his lordship above all things to be mistaken for a
coachman by calling.

Moreover, the streets resounded through the
day with the cries of those who hawked their
wares ; such cries being in general musical in
their long-sustained cadence, though not always
intelligible to the ear.

A writer of "An Examination of Certain
Abuses, Corruptions, and Enormities in the
City of Dublin," declares he cannot have a
minute's ease or patience until he has exposed
the same. One of his grievances is that persons of both sex who cry through the streets
the necessaries of life, are not readily under-
standable. "I would," he says, "advise all
new-comers to look out at their garret windows,
and there see whether the thing that is cried
be tripes or flummery buttermilk or cowheels.
For as things are now managed, how is it
possible for an honest countryman just arrived
to find out what is meant, for instance, by
the following words, with which his ears are con-

stantly stunned twice a day: 'Muggs, juggs, and porringers, up in the garret and down in the cellar'? I say how is it possible for any stranger to understand that this jargon is meant as an invitation to buy a farthing's worth of milk for his breakfast or supper, unless his curiosity draws him to the window, or till his landlady shall inform him?"

The streets were unguarded by day, and for many years in the beginning of the eighteenth century, by night likewise, until they became unsafe for all peace-loving people. So frequent were these scenes of violence, abuse and robbery, that during the existence of the Volunteers a body of those gentlemen arranged amongst themselves to guard the streets by night, and protect honest folk who were compelled by necessity to venture abroad. But this self-constituted guard soon fell away from its prescribed duties, and in 1723 an Act was passed under which the different parishes were required to appoint "honest men and good Protestants" to be night-watchers of the city. Those who most frequently disturbed the peace were the two hundred hackney coachmen, who, with their rivals of equal

number, the public chair-men, were continually
arguing, threatening, drinking, and fighting ; a
roystering uncouth lot for the benefit of whose
soul and body the magistrates were continually
inflicting chastisement of half-a-crown fines, or
in case of an offender being unable to pay the
same, of sending him to the House of Correction,
there to be whipped and kept at hard labour
for a time not exceeding twenty-four hours.

The beggars of the city were a numerous
body in themselves, picturesque in their rags,
content in their sordidness, frequently turbu-
lent, fantastic in their manners, humorous and
eloquent in their speech, cheerful when relieved
of their wants, stoical in their indifference to
privations ; philosophers all, who put into
practice the national idea that to live without
work was the highest wealth, and the greatest
happiness was the enjoyment of freedom.
Amongst them was old Tim Rogers, a red-faced
man with shrewd eyes, " an' the smallest taste
of a nose, for all the world as if 'twas flung at
his face and remained there." His tormentors
and detractors, whom he styled " the purty
boys," and " the Dublin Jackeens," used to say

that for years he represented himself as being dumb, and wore a card on his breast that bespoke such affliction, until one evening, "having a sup in," he betrayed his secret; for on being asked by someone in the same jovial condition as himself, how long he had been dumb, he replied, "Four year come St. John's Eve, plaze yer honour."

Be that as it may, his tongue was shrewd and sharp enough now. "Plaze your honour," he would say to any well-dressed stranger who noticed him, his manner quite confidential and polite, " It's what I'm going to ask you for a penny piece, because I'd sooner trouble you nor any man in all Ireland, on account of your elegant character. An' sure enough these are the worst times I ever remember either afore or since I was born." If entered into conversation with, he was ready to relate that, "If it wasn't for Crummel and his murtherin' troopers, bad luck to their sowls, the rascals, for they tuck me grandfather's property, ay, an' his grandfather's property afore him—if it wasn't for them, I say, it's drivin' in me carriage I'd be this very day, glory be to God ; but sure, as it

is I'm owld and helpless an' I'm nearly kilt with
the hunger, so give me a penny piece to bury
me." More than a penny piece to Tim Rogers
was a glass of whisky, which he liked strong,
being a connoisseur of the beverage ; and once he
was known to rebuke one who offered him whisky
that lacked that quality, " Now, avourneen," says
he, " wouldn't it be a mighty fine thing if they'd
take the duty off whisky and put it on water ? "

Katty Clare, who dressed in a dark red cloak
and had a taste for finery, with which she
adorned her person, was another notable figure,
fluent in speech, persuasive, humorous, with the
natural love of acting dominating her. One
day when Delane and his fellow-player
Sparks were coming down Essex Street, the
latter met an acquaintance to whom he stopped
to talk, whilst Delane moved on a few paces
before pausing to await his friend. Katty
Clare went up to Sparks, and heedless of inter-
rupting him, began to beg.

"O lave the poor woman a penny, an'
may the blessin' o' God follow you all your
life."

" I have nothing for you."

"Give me a penny, an' may you never want a friend as I do."

"I told you I have nothing for you."

"Arrah, God forbid that you should have nothing, sure it's yourself has plenty. Give me a penny, an' may the blessin' o' God follow you all the days of your life."

"Go to the devil," cried Sparks in a rage.

"O' thin, may it never overtake you," says Katty Clare.

Away she went to Delane, and began with him.

"Give the poor woman a penny for the love an' honour o' God."

"Now why do you come to me?" he asked.

"Sure, Mr. Sparks sent me to the devil, an' I came straight to your honour," she answered gravely.

Delane burst out laughing.

"Faith and troth, it's aisy to know a rale gentleman," she began coaxingly.

"How do you get your living?" he asked.

"Me livin', is it? Arrah, honey," she replied, "I takes what God sends me. It's that unlucky I am that I've lost me father, so I'm an orphan, for I've only a mother, and never a brother or sister but meself."

"But, my good woman, you are young and strong, why don't you work?" suggested the actor.

"Me dear joy," she answered, "sure it's not wantin' me to be a worker you'd be. Faith, I'd rather be a player, like yourself."

Nothing pleased her better, poor soul, than to hold discourse with "the rale gentry," and she never lost an opportunity of speaking to them. One morning, whilst Lord and Lady Desart were waiting in their carriage outside the office of the *Dublin Intelligence* until a copy of that sheet was printed, Katty came up smiling and courtesying to them, at once familiar and subservient.

"Ah, me lady, success to your ladyship, and success to your lordship's honour, this morning of all the blessed mornings in the year," she began.

"Why this morning?" Lady Desart inquired

"Sure, didn't I dream last night that you ladyship gave me a pound o' tay and his lord ship gave me a pound o' tabacca," she answered.

"But don't you know that dreams always go by the contrary?" Lord Desart asked.

"Do they, plaze your lordship?" she asked in her gravest manner. "Then in that case it must be your lordship that will give me the tay, an' her ladyship that will give me the tabacca."

The most notable of all the Dublin mendicants was a poor paralyzed cripple named Hackball, or "the king of the beggars," who was drawn daily in a small car by two great dogs to his post on the Old Bridge. "It's six miles a day the bastes carry me," he once said to a stranger who admired the dogs, "but as there's two of 'em, sure it's only three miles apiece." One day, when a troop of horse passed over the bridge, a young lad who had been playing in the centre was knocked down and ridden over. A score of sympathizers ran to pick him up when the dashing soldiers had gone, and to the surprise of all the boy had escaped unhurt.

"Go down on yer knees, you reprobate, and thank God you're left alive," cried an old woman.

"Arrah, what would you have him thank

36

God for?" asked Hackball. "Is it for letting a troop of horse run over him?"

He could be satirical on occasions, as those who refused him charity discovered. One day, when Colonel MacGrath, who was famed for his ugliness, remained deaf to Hackball's entreaties, the cripple said: "Well, sure God Almighty will never let your honour fall in a duel, anyway."

"How is that?" asked the gallant man, who became interested in the prediction.

"Sure your face would frighten the bravest man out o' the field, me honey," the beggar exclaimed.

He was likewise something of a philosopher, and when coppers were few he would comfort himself with the reflection, "Ah, thin, money is the divil's own, and God keeps it from us; an' that's the raison the people of Ireland are vartuous beyond description."

These same streets presented some strange scenes by day, as may be gathered from the news' sheets of the period. Here, for instance, in Fishamble Street five stout bailiffs, armed with blunderbusses, lie in wait for Captain

French, whose hospitality had encumbered his estates and covered him with debt; but no sooner had they pounced upon this gallant man than he knocked some of them down and cut and bruised the others as he made his escape. "And it is to be observed," quaintly remarks the *Dublin Journal*, "that those who were esteemed the most courageous amongst them, lay sprawling on the ground and suffered the gentleman to walk over them in his flight." In recording one of the common attempts at roguery in the streets by night, the *Dublin Advertiser*, of October, 1736, quaintly adds: " This notice, like all others in our paper, is to let the town know that street robbers are abroad, and that gentlemen who go home late, should be cautioned of them."

Scarce a day passed that someone was not placed in the pillory, for some social offence, such persons being called by the crowd "the babes in the wood." Occasionally women were burned for the murder of their infants: and it was not an uncommon thing for the usual routine of street life to be disturbed by a strange procession, headed perhaps by Crazy Crow, who had been imprisoned for stealing bodies from St. Andrew's churchyard, and consisting of unwashed children, street boys, and other idlers, who, cheering, scoffing and jesting, voluntarily escorted women who were being whipped through the city for keeping disorderly houses. Wayfarers passing the city Marshalsea on Merchants' Quay were incessantly assailed by the pitiful cries, and hands outstretched through iron bars, of the inmates imprisoned for debt, who solicited charity for their maintenance, or for the discharge of their fees.

Those who at night passed this same place, which received debtors and malefactors alike, occasionally heard stranger, weirder, and sadder sounds. Such sounds as ribald songs, the oaths of card-players, and the laughter of drunkards, when they who heard, knew that some convict doomed to execution next morning was being "waked" by his friends, who had probably robbed, begged or pawned that they might gain admission to the prison by bribery of the jailor, and buy whisky that the criminal's last night might be made as merry as possible.

It was not merely robbery which was to be

39

dreaded in the streets at night, but violence,
some of those who were merry in their cups
being anxious to divert themselves on their
homeward way by picking a quarrel or knock-
ing a man down. And wherever there was a
group of chair-men, there was sure to be a
squabble between them, or with some passer-by,
on whom they were ready to pour a fire of
comments, the sparks of their wit being sure
to smart. Those whose business took them to
Cork Hill were certain to be molested or
insulted by such fellows who in vast numbers
waited outside Lucas's, with whom it was never
safe to enter into competition; for the coffee-
house waiters invariably took sides with the
chair-men, and from the windows flung bucket-
fuls of foul water on all who might retaliate.

The numerous clubhouses of the city swarmed
with men of the first distinction, who here
sought excitement in card-playing, duelling, or
dice, or who desired to draw near each other
in bonds of comradeship; whilst wine taverns
and coffee houses, each with its painted sign
swinging above the portal, were centres where
persons of wit, political pamphleteers, lam-

pooners, and lovers of the play congregated to
hear, to impart, or to invent news. Each coffee
house had its own set of frequenters. The
Globe in Essex Street was the resort of
University dons, lawyers and physicians. The
players found their way to a tavern at the
corner of Temple Lane, known to them as the
House of Lords, from the fact that its proprietor
was named Ben Lord. At Jack's coffee house
on College Green might be met such writers
and men of talent as Robert Lord Molesworth,
who from being the son of a Dublin merchant,
was made a member of the Privy Council by
King William, and by him sent as ambassador
to Denmark, of which country he wrote a
history held in much esteem ; and Sir Thomas
Molyneaux, who published various tracts on
physic and botany and the natural history of
Ireland ; and Thomas Southerne, who wrote ten
dramatic pieces, amongst which Isabella and
Oronooka were said to rank after Shakespeare
and Otway in dramatic effect ; and Dean Swift,
who was worshipped by the people and followed
by crowds when he walked abroad ; and
Thomas Parnell, wit, poet, and biographer, who

had a living at Finglass; and Marmaduke
Coghil, a doctor of civil law who afterwards
became Chancellor of the Irish Exchequer;
and other learned men, all in themselves
excellent company.

Lucas's coffee house on Cork Hill was a
famous resort for young bloods and men of
fashion; for here was not only the certainty of
hearing the latest news concerning politics and
plays, but there was a possibility of experiencing
the pleasant excitement of witnessing a duel.
For combats between men of honour and
renown frequently occurred in the yard, when
the company assembled in the coffee house
would flock to the windows to lay wagers on
the probable survivors, and see that the laws
of honour were preserved. Amongst the most
noted of those who resorted to Lucas's was
Talbot Edgeworth, an eccentric youth who
"thought of nothing but fine clothes and
splendid furniture for his horse," and flattered
himself that he excited universal admiration.
So long as his appearance was as resplendent as
satin and lace, jewels and embroideries, could
make it, he cared not how he lived; nor was

his extravagance designed to bring him the favours of the opposite sex; for 'twas his common phrase that they "Might look and die." "To do him justice," writes one of his contemporaries, "he was an exceedingly handsome fellow, well shaped and of good height, rather tall than of middle size. He began very early in his life, even before he was of age, to shine forth in the world. He bethought himself very happily of one extravagance well suited to his disposition; he insisted upon an exclusive right to one board at Lucas's coffee house, where he might walk backwards and forwards and exhibit himself to the gaze of all beholders, in which particular he was indulged almost universally; but now and then some arch fellow would usurp on his privilege, take possession of the board, meet him and dispute his right; and when this happened to be the case, he would chafe, bluster, ask the gentleman his name, and immediately set him down in his table book as a man he would fight when he came to age."

The Hellfire Club, of which Lord Rosse was supposed to be the founder, held its meetings in a tavern situated in Sau's Court, Fishamble Street, and was distinguished for its "unlicensed and disgraceful orgies and brutalities, and its indulgence in riot and every species of violence —all that the devil would do if run stark mad, and to an extent that would now appear incredible." On one occasion it pleased the members of this club to seize upon a chair-man, and binding him, to force down his throat as much whisky as he could hold, as he lay upon his back. When his mouth began to overflow with the liquid it was set on fire, much to their amusement. The chair-man died, and the leading spirit of this adventure, my Lord Santry, was brought to trial, convicted and sentenced to death. Immense interest was used to save him from the gallows, and it was said the Government was finally induced to pardon him because of the threat made by his uncle, Sir Compton Domville, of Temple Square, that if the execution took place he would deprive the city of water, the supply of which was situated on his property.

Though my Lord Santry's life was spared by man, its course was not prolonged by God, for in the *Dublin Journal* of May 5th, 1737, we read that " He hath ordered all his tradesmen to send in their bills, that they may be paid off. His lordship is much indisposed, and continues to behave himself with the greatest con- trition."

Not far from Lucas's was Swan Alley, where gambling-houses abounded notwithstanding that raids were frequently made on them by the watch, and their tables publicly burned by order of the Lord Mayor. Then on Cork Hill was the Cockpit Royal where cock-fighting flourished. The battles, which were attended by men of the first quality, youths with more money than brains, and a concourse of the city rabble, usually began at noon. The greatest excite- ment was felt by all witnesses, and the betting generally ran for about forty guineas a battle, and five hundred guineas for the main, or odd battle; but at times thousands of guineas changed hands in consequence of the triumph or defeat of a cock.

The most remarkable practice in the social life of the day was duelling. In no other capital of Europe was the habit so common, the reasons for which are not far to seek. Though in vogue before the battle of the Boyne, it was not until after that event had ended that duelling became a universal usage amongst men of quality in Ireland. The battle being lost and won, the dissolution of the Irish army followed, when a number of military men were drifted all over the country, who, whilst without employment or means of living, were sensitively tenacious of their rank and feelings as gentlemen, and readily susceptible to slights or insults, which they were quick to resent by swords or pistols. On the other hand, the soldiers of the Williamite army were not apt to respect or consider those who had ruined themselves by adhesion to the cause of James II. And on either side were temperaments hot, irritable, and hostile, which coming into constant collision, established a practice of prompt resentment that soon spread to the more peaceful classes.

In a little while it therefore came to be considered that a course of duelling was an essential part of a young man's education, a test of character, a sign of spirit, and indeed was not regarded as a cause for future enmity between surviving combatants, but frequently proved a means of cementing friendship. The clergy were perhaps the only men laying claim to gentle blood who did not enter the field ; several Irish judges had, whilst holding that high office, "smelt powder," while a certain Provost of Trinity College, the Rev. Hely Hutchinson, had once upon a time fought Mr. Doyle, a Master of Chancery ; and the Right Hon. George Ogle, a Privy Councillor, had fought Barney Coyle, a distiller, for no other reason than because he was a Papist.

Shooting galleries were plentiful enough in the city, where men resorted to fire at a mark when antagonists were unfortunately few ; and many of the gun makers accommodated their customers by allowing them to shoot in the yards behind, or the cellars beneath their shops. It was in a cellar of Muley's, of Dame Street, that Nicholas French snuffed a candle at twelve yards a dozen times in succession, though his skill did not prevent him from being shot dead in a duel by a man who had never before been out.

Combats were occasionally the result of the slightest causes ; sometimes, indeed, they were fought whilst one of the duellists remained in ignorance of the offence for which he was called upon to pay with his life. But no gentleman of spirit wished to keep "the irons idle," and the more duels he survived, the greater his pride. One who was of this way of thinking, Major Forbes, nearly shot poor Lord Trimlestown before his lordship was even aware of his danger.

And it happened in this way.

Lord Trimlestown, a thoughtful and studious man, who had studied medicine abroad, and cured the poor at home free of charge, was reading in a summer-house attached to his residence in Clontarf, a suburb of Dublin, when he was suddenly alarmed by hearing a couple of bullets whiz past him, not three inches from his head, they having been sent through the door. Rising in alarm, he looked out of a window and saw two gentlemen who were just charging their pistols again, as he rightly supposed, to hit some mark on the door, on which he rushed out and in the civilest manner possible remonstrated with them for their rashness in firing at the summer-house without first ascertaining if any one were inside.

48

"Sir," said the major, seeing a mighty fine opportunity for a fight, "I didn't know you were within there, and I don't now know who in the world you may be; but if I have given offence I'm entirely willing to offer you the satisfaction of a gentleman, so take your choice," and he held out two pistols.

His lordship took hold of both pistols, and with a twinkle in his eyes made answer, "Do me the justice, sir, to enter the summer-house, shut the door, and let me have two shots at you, then we shall be on equal terms, and I shall be quite at your service to give or to receive the satisfaction of a gentleman."

This ready reply, and the manner in which it was made, not only appeased but pleased the Major, who said, "Upon my conscience, sir, I believe you are a very honest fellow, and I have a great mind to shake hands with you. Will you only tell me who you are?"

Lord Trimlestown, who was known far and wide as one who freely gave his substance and his services to all who asked, mentioned his name.

"I beg your lordship's pardon," said the

Major, "and sure that's what no man ever accused me of doing before; and had I known who you were I would as soon have shot my own soul and body as have fired at the door. But how could I tell who was inside?"

"That's the very thing of which I have to complain," said his lordship, laughingly, when he shook hands with the good-hearted fellow who had nearly shot him, and offered him the hospitalities of his house, which were readily accepted.

As an illustration of the light manner in which duels were frequently provoked and the friendships they begot, that fought by Mr. Mathew may be mentioned. Two gentlemen, Major Pack and Captain Creed, came out of England to seek adventure in this way, they being men of courage and experts with the sword. No sooner had they arrived in Dublin, than making inquiries, they heard that a certain Mr. Mathew, a person of good estate and hospitable nature, who had lately arrived from France, bore the character of being the first swordsman in Europe.

With him Pack accordingly resolved to pick

a quarrel. So seeing him as he was being conveyed in his chair, Pack jostled the fore carrier. Supposing this to be accidental, Mathew took no notice of the circumstance ; but Pack, repairing to a public coffee house, boasted that he had purposely offered an insult to Mathew, who had not the spirit to resent it. Now at that moment there happened to be present a particular friend of Mathew's named Macnamara, himself a fencer of courage and renown, who, taking up the quarrel, said he was sure Mr. Mathew suspected no affront, or the offender would have been chastised upon the spot, but if the Major would let him know where he might be found, immediately on the return of his friend, who was dining that day a little out of town, the speaker would call upon him.

The Major willingly named Lucas's coffee house where he and a friend would await Macnamara's commands. And no sooner had Mathew returned and been made aware of what had passed, than, accompanied by his henchman, he gaily hied him to the tavern in question. Being shown into the room where Pack and Creed were, the latter, after securing the door, drew their swords without expostulation or excuse, but Macnamara stopped them, saying he had something to propose ; " For," said he, " in cases of this matter I could never be a cool spectator, and if you please, sir," he added, turning to Creed, " I shall have the honour of entertaining you in the same manner."

And Creed desiring no better sport, they drew their swords, all four of them setting to work with perfect composure and elegant skill. For awhile the conflict seemed even, but soon the officers began to lose blood, and later it became evident they were no match for their antagonists. The first to fall was Creed, upon which Pack called out, "Ah, poor Creed, are you gone ? " "Yes," replied Mathew, " and you shall instantly pack after him." Saying which he ran him through the body. Though the number of wounds received by the vanquished was great, their opponents were untouched. Surgeons were hastily summoned, and it was feared that Pack and Creed must die ; beds were brought into the room where they had fought, and all assistance rendered them. When after some hours they regained their senses, Pack in a feeble voice said to his companion, "Creed, I think we are the conquerors, for we have kept the field of battle."

When after many days they were permitted to see company, Mathew and his friend attended them constantly; and from this companionship a close intimacy afterwards ensued.

CHAPTER III.

Public spectacles—Receiving the Viceroy—A gorgeous spectacle—King William's statue—Dining with the Lord Lieutenant on Twelfth Day—A strange custom —Places of recreation—Some eccentric characters —A wise woman—An Irish lord at home—Lord Rosse and his practical joke.

THE population of the capital, at this time estimated at a hundred and fifty thousand, was continually gratified with public spectacles, the pomp and circumstance of which feasted their eyes, the colour, display, and grace of which appealed to imaginations that would have been as vivid, luxurious, and sensuous as those of Oriental peoples, but for the perpetual gloom of the skies that overshadowed and the mournful rhythm of the seas that surround this isle.

Amongst such spectacles was the entrance of the Viceroy—frequently changed in days of political uncertainty—into the kingdom he was to govern. On the signal being given of his arrival in Dublin Bay, the Privy Council, Judges, Officers of State and of the Household, together with the nobility, hastened to the sea shore in coaches outnumbering three hundred, not to speak of troops of horsemen, whilst the throng of the populace on such occasions was prodigious ; they presently holding on to the wheels and trappings of the coaches containing the Lord Lieutenant and his suite, so that the journey to the Castle, which could have been made in thirty minutes, generally occupied four hours. Then at night great and small guns were fired, bonfires made the streets luminous, whilst wine and ale were freely given to the people at the expense of the Primate and the nobility.

The procession of the Trades was a spectacle that caused the greatest excitement of all, and was witnessed once every three years, when people not only from the provinces, but from England and France, assembled to enjoy the sight. According to the terms of their charter, the Corporation were bound to perambulate the limits of the Lord Mayor's jurisdiction, to make stands at various points, and to skirt the

Liberties of the Earl of Meath, a district then quite distinct from the city of Dublin proper.

These processions, which were held on the first day of August, were not only composed of the Lord Mayor and Corporation, but of the various trade guilds, which were twenty-five in number ; each having its masters, journeymen, and apprentices, its badges, banners, and patrons. Each trade of course strove to outshine the other in colour and display ; all of them having immense platforms with high canopies, gilded, decorated with ribbons and flowers, and drawn by six richly-bedecked horses. These platforms were fitted as workshops whereon the respective trades were exhibited ; the printers striking off merry songs and odes to the Lord Mayor, which they flung into the air ; the tanners, dressed in sheep and goat skins, at work upon leather ; the apothecaries compounding pills, which they showered upon the throng ; the silk-weavers making ribbons ; the vintners dressed like Bacchus, drinking healths ; the fishmongers exhibiting twelve good men representing the apostles. Behind these cars came the masters on splendid horses handsomely caparisoned, followed by the journeymen on foot, they in turn succeeded by the apprentices, a formidable body ; bands playing, people cheering, crowds swaying, gilding and harness and armour glinting in the August sun, the sound of bells in the air.

On coming to the Earl of Meath's Liberties, a prearranged scene took place. The Liberties consisted of an elevated tract on the western side of the city, so-called from certain privileges and immunities conferred upon its inhabitants. These were the descendants of a number of French artisans who after the revocation of the Edict of Nantz had settled here, where they had brought the manufacture of silk and woollens to the highest state of perfection. For generations they, having intermarried, preserved the same facial type and distinct characteristics of their race, and were a people apart from the general body of citizens. Possessing their own manor courts and seneschals, with a courthouse and a prison, they were jealous of their rights of separate jurisdiction. Therefore when my Lord Mayor and his sword-bearer approached the boundaries, their progress was stopped by the denizens of the Liberties, and a formidable show of resistance made, for wherever his lordship was permitted to walk, there would his jurisdiction reach. And when in the course of the day's procession the Lord Mayor came to the North Wall, he and his attendants got into a gorgeously-decorated barge in which they were rowed out into the bay. There, his lordship standing up, threw a dart with all his force, and where it fell a buoy was fixed, and so far would his warrant have power over all vessels that anchored between the city and that spot. On such days all business was suspended, enjoyment was the pursuit of the hour, and the crowds in every street were so great that you could have walked over the heads of men, women, and children all eager to enjoy the sight.

Other processions not popular with the vast mass of the population were those which made a circuit on the 12th of July and 4th of November, the anniversaries of the Battle of the Boyne and the birthday of King William, around the equestrian statue of his Majesty in College Green; the effigy on such occasions being dressed in a flaming cloak and sash, and decorated with orange lilies, the horse made splendid with ribbons of the same colour, whilst beneath his upraised foot were ribbons of the national colour, on which he was ready to trample. Since the statue had been erected on the 1st of July, 1701, this object of political idolatry had had great homage paid it for many years ; for not only were all who passed it on the days mentioned expected to salute the image with lifted hat, but on such dates a procession consisting of the Viceroy, the Primate, the Lord Mayor, Sheriffs, and Aldermen, the Provost of Trinity College, judges and officers of the Revenue, the different bodies of volunteers of Dublin city and county, all arrayed in ceremonial robes and their suitable uniforms, solemnly walked round it thrice to the beating of drums, the ringing of bells, and the firing of cannon, flags flying and sabres gleaming ; whilst at night, according to the *Dublin Intelligencer*, the festivities concluded " with an illumination or bonfire or riot and other demonstrations of joy."

In the *Dublin Daily Advertiser* of November 5th, 1731, we read : " Yesterday being the anniversary of our Great Deliverer, the Constable of St. Andrew's Watch on duty, being a very

loyal man, made a bonfire before the effigie of
King William on College Green and set candles
all round the Reals (rails), and candles in
lanthorns above where the horse stands, which
made a glorious show; then paraded his men,
which were thirty in number, and he at the
head of them, with an orange sash and cockade,
and a half pike in his hand. He drank the
immortal memory of King William and made
all his men do the same. Then he marched
them in ranks four men deep, with their candles
lighted in their lanthorns and borne upon the
tops of their watch poles, which made a most
agreeable sight. The procession was carryed
on with decency and order, and closed with
hussaws of joy and approbation. At his return
he and his men drank their Majesties' healths
and all the Royal Family."

The Jacobite spirit occasionally showed itself
by maltreating and disfiguring the statue,
decorating it with green boughs, and setting a
straw figure behind his glorious Majesty, who
was thus wickedly mocked. The offenders
were not unfrequently the students of Trinity
College, being led to such bold outrages by the

shade of their politics, the love of mischief, and their desire to revenge the offence offered the university by the image turning his back upon the building. In 1710 three youths were expelled from the university and sentenced to six months imprisonment, having first been led to College Green, there to stand before the statue for half an hour with the inscription on their breasts, " I stand here for defacing the statue of our glorious deliverer, the late King William," and to pay the sum of one hundred pounds each. A petition had the effect of saving them from the former humiliation and of reducing the fine to five shillings.

Four years after, " some profligate persons, disaffected to his Majesty's Government, did in the night time offer great indignities to the memory of King William by taking out and breaking the truncheon in his statue." Though Government offered a hundred pounds for their conviction, those wicked men were never discovered. This outrage was again perpetrated some years later, whilst towards the end of the century, in 1798, one Walter Cox, by trade a gunsmith, actually attempted to decapitate his Majesty by filing at his neck.

Though these processions kept party feeling aglow and caused bitter animosity, they were not discontinued until 1805, when the Duke of Bedford, then Lord-Lieutenant, refused to sanction such proceedings by his presence; but the statue was still decorated for many years subsequently.

The rancour that found vent in such exhibitions was mainly sustained by the various Orange Societies established throughout the city. Concerning the first of these ever formed, which called itself "The Aldermen of Skinners Alley," Sir Jonah Barrington, who became a member, gives us some details. Its orirginal members had consisted of the Aldermen whom James II. had disbanded but whom William had reinstated. The organization had undergone little alteration for near a century previous to the date Barrington joined.

Its chief object was to honour the memory of William of Orange and to combat papacy; and to make its influence the wider its number was unlimited, and its members embraced men of all classes, so that general officers and wig-makers, king's counsel and lawyers' clerks, were alike heartily welcomed to its ranks. The fees were sixpence a month, a sum which, allowing for absentees, afforded plenty of eatables, porter and punch, for those who attended the monthly dinners.

The great feast of the year, however, was held on the anniversary of the battle of the Boyne, when the standing dish was sheep's trotters, a delicate allusion to King James's running away from Ireland. Rum punch in plenty filled the blue jugs, whisky-punch the white jugs, whilst porter foamed in the pewter measures scattered over the table. In the midst, solemnly surveying the scene, was a bust of King William, that was "regarded as a sort of deity."

Midway through dinner the toast was given, which, stripped of its more offensive phrases, ran as follows :—

" The glorious, pious, and immortal memory of the great and good King William ; not forgetting Oliver Cromwell, who assisted in redeeming us from popery, slavery, arbitrary power, brass money, and wooden shoes. May we never want a Williamite to kick a Jacobite, or a rope for the Bishop of Cork. And he that won't drink this, whether he be priest, bishop, deacon, bellows-blower, or grave-digger, may a north wind blow him to the south, and a west wind blow him to the east. May Cerberus make a meal of him, and Pluto a snuff-box of his skull. Amen." Then every man present, having unbuttoned the knees of his breeches, drank this toast on his bare joints with the utmost enthusiasm; after which all rising and seating themselves continued their meal, when the punch passed more rapidly and the spirit of loyalty increased by what it supped on.

One of the members of this club was an apothecary named M'Mahon, who, though he secretly had leanings towards papacy, professed Orangism that he might the better prosper in his trade. For awhile he was able to keep his private sentiments to himself, until at one unlucky dinner of the society he drank too deeply from the blue jug, when he began to speak irreverently of Dutch William.

" His worthy associates," writes Sir Jonah, "took fire at this sacrilege offered to their patron saint; and one word brought on another. M'Mahon grew outrageous, and in his paroxysm actually damned King William. In the enthusiasm of his popery, and most thoughtlessly for himself and for the unhappy king's bust then standing before him, he struck it with his huge fist plump in the face.

"The bust immediately showed evident symptoms of maltreatment; its white marble appearing to be actually stained with blood. One of the aldermen roared out 'That villain M'Mahon has broken the king's nose.' 'The king's nose,' ran through the room; the cry of 'Throw him out of the window' was unanimously adopted; the window was opened, and M'Mahon, after exercising all his muscular powers, forced out remorselessly. Again the Glorious Memory was drunk, the king's nose washed clean from the blood formerly belonging to M'Mahon's knuckles, and all restored to peace and tranquillity.

"Fortunately for M'Mahon a lamp and lamp iron stood immediately under the window. His route downwards was impeded by a crash against the lamp; the glass and other materials yielded to the precious weight, and probably prevented the pavement from having the honour of braining him. He held a moment by the iron, and then dropped quite gently into the arms of a couple of guardians of the night, who, attracted by the uproar in the room above, and seeing M'Mahon getting out feet foremost, conceived that it was only a drunken frolic, and so placed themselves underneath ' to keep the gentleman out of the gutter.' "

A sight which annually diverted the town was the procession of the Lord Mayor, Sheriffs, and Aldermen in their huge coaches, most richly decorated, with servants and coachmen in handsome liveries, that drove on twelfth day to dine with the Lord-Lieutenant.

The dinner, which was attended with much ceremony, consisted merely of two courses, after which dessert was placed upon the table. Then his Excellency called for servers of wine, he being first helped by a page, and all the company having their glasses filled, the Lord-Lieutenant rose, as did the company and drank loyal toasts, including " The Glorious Memory of King William."

Then grace was said, the Viceroy rose and recommended his guests to the care of the steward, comptroller, and gentleman usher, who gravely conducted the city fathers from the dining-room down to the cellar, where was a table with glasses, when each guest tasted what hogshead he pleased. The effect did not invariably tend towards dignity. On one occasion "some being thus drinking in the cellar and dwelling longer on the wine than usual, sent to the Lord-Lieutenant asking him to order them chairs, who returned for answer that he could not encourage any gentleman's drinking longer than he could stand." This curious custom of visiting the cellar was continued until 1762.

Public promenades, where the gentry took the air, were numerous enough; the water-works in St. James's Street being a favourite resort, here being a great basin from whence, by pipes, the city was supplied by water, pleasant green walks surrounding it. In the Deer Park, now known as Phœnix Park, was a vast ring round which they drove in fine weather. Then St. Stephen's Green was a site where the nobility of both sexes made a gay appearance. But perhaps the most favourite walk was the Strand—in other words, the sea-shore—"which in bright and serene weather gives a delightful prospect by the sailing inwards and outwards of shipping; also to the mountains of Wicklow and the Hill of Howth ; and as the shore is level for seven or eight miles, it is much resorted to by all degrees of persons."

All kinds of manly exercises, sports, recreations and vices were carried on, such as back sword, cudgels, boxing and wrestling, bull-baiting, cock-fighting, hunting, coursing, hawking, setting, fishing, fowling, cards, dice, billiards, balls, plays, consorts of music, singing, dancing, women and wine ; for Dublin was gay and given to dissipation.

The city had many notable "karacters" whose appearance or actions afforded vast diversion. There was Captain Debrisay, for nstance, a gracious and eccentric man, who dressed after the fashion of the seventeenth century ; a great cocked hat on one side of his head nearly covering his left eye, a powdered wig hanging in curls, at the back a black cockade with a small curl depending, his waistcoat reaching to his knees, open except at the last button, that the wealth of his frills might be seen.   Then there was Dr. John Rulby, the Quaker, a celebrated naturalist, who was so strongly persuaded that the Old Bridge would fall whilst he was crossing, that for thirty years he inconvenienced himself greatly rather than use it.

The Reverend Robert Master furnished much diversion, for he could prove to his own satisfaction that the 25th of December was not the anniversary of Christ's birth, it being a popish superstition, foolishly and fondly imagined, to fix it upon that date.   And sure wasn't Counsellor Peter Daly himself a wonderful man, for his tongue had won him a great fortune that enabled him to marry his daughters three to real lords, to wit, the Earls of Howth and Kerry, and Viscount Kingsland.   A greater favourite with the town was Sir Toby Butler, a mighty eloquent man, who could make his wit and his sarcasm equally felt, and who invariably drank his bottle of claret before going to the courts.   One day when a client who was most anxious about the success of his case besought Sir Toby to forego his usual custom, the lawyer promised on his honour he would not drink his bottle that morning. He went to the court, pleaded his case in rare style, and gained his verdict. The client, wringing Sir Toby's hands in delight, pointed out the virtue of abstinence.

" Why," replied Sir Toby, " if I hadn't taken the bottle I should have lost the case."

" But your promise ? " said the client, a little crestfallen.

" I kept it faithfully and honourably," answered the lawyer ; " I did not drink a drop ; I merely poured my bottle of claret into a wheaten loaf and ate it ; so I had my bottle and you had your verdict, and I remain a man of my word."

Amongst other notable characters were John Whalley and Andrew Crumpsty, astrologers, and Nanny Morrisey, the " Culloch " or wise woman.

As may be supposed from the strain of mysticism, from the love of the supernatural, from a belief in the unseen which are dominant characteristics in a spiritualized and impressionable people, that necromancers, astrologers, and wise men had flourished in the island for centuries. Sir John Harrington, writing in the reign of Elizabeth, says that English soldiers were daunted by the belief that the Irish possessed magical powers, and remarks that it was a general practice amongst them "to charm girdles and the like, persuading men that while they wear them they cannot be hurt by any weapon." The race of necromancers and astrologers in the beginning of the eighteenth century was not only represented by Whalley and Crumpsty, but likewise by one Harvey, a man tall in stature, round-shouldered, pale-visaged, ferret-eyed, who was never seen to laugh. This individual, who was said to work charms and conjure spirits, is described in 1728 as being unalterable in regard of dress, which he would not have changed to prevent a plague or a famine. "On his head was a broad slouching hat and white cap, about his neck was tied a broad band with tassels hanging down. He wore a long dangling coat of good broadcloth, close breasted, and buttoned from top to bottom; no skirts, no waistcoat ; a pair of trouse-breeches down to his ankles ; broad-toed, low-heeled shoes, which were a novelty in his time, and the latchets tied with two pack threads ; a long black stick, no gloves ; and thus, bending nearly double, he trudged slowly along the streets with downcast eyes, minding nobody, but still muttering something to himself."

Professor John Whalley, who lived next door to the Wheel of Fortune Tavern, on the west side of Stephen's Green, compiled prophetic almanacks which contained "advice from the stars," compounded medicines to cure all diseases, and consulted the planets regarding the affairs of daily life. By some he was called a quack ; by others he was supposed to hold converse with the devil ; but be that as it may, many thronged to ask advice from him. Andrew Crumpsty he regarded with wrath as a pretender to knowledge of a divine science, who really " knew no more of genuine astrology than one of his brethren which are usually plac't in perriwig-makers' windows," and Crumpsty was moreover "a mathemaggoty monster."

Nanny Morrisey lived in Skinners Alley—a

wrinkled-faced, dark-eyed, toothless old woman,
who was learned in the virtues of herbs and
simples, which she gathered at various seasons
under the rising of certain planets with many
a rhythmic incantation and many a muttered
charm. Not only did the poor flock to her, but
likewise people of quality whom the medical
faculty had been unable to cure by purging or
bleeding ; and it was Nanny's opinion, freely
given, that "docthers and 'pothecaries atween
them, kills more people than you'd pass in a
day's walk, glory be to God."

Lord Eyre of Eyre Court, who frequently
visited Dublin but had never been out of Ireland
in his life, was a well-known figure. The greater
part of the year was spent in his own spacious
mansion, which, though a trifle out of repair, he
made no effort to renovate. Like most of his
class at this period, his house was opened to all
who desired to claim its hospitality ; his table
groaned with superabundance, and in his kitchen
usually hung a roasted ox, from which a great
retinue of servitors helped themselves at pleasure
by slicing what they needed from the carcase.
His lordship, who had no leisure to look after

73

his vast lands, the greater part of which lay waste and unproductive, hunted the fox in season and was a great lover of cock-fighting. When at home, he dined at three o'clock, and for the remainder of the day never left his table or the company surrounding it, who drank claret till they could drink no more. He never read books or news-sheets, he had little curiosity regarding events which moved the world, and he had no great liking for fresh air, for not a window in his house was made to open, though the glass in several was smashed. Amongst his retainers were his pipers, who at certain hours of the evening did not always play in harmony, and his runners, who were " the smartest boys in the whole country round," and his cock-feeders, who flung oatmeal into the air as thanksgiving offer-ings to unseen powers when his lordship's birds were victorious in battle.

But amongst the most merry of his time was Richard Parsons, created Earl of Rosse in 1718. His fund of wit was infinite, his heart was generous to all, and his love of pleasure was inordinate. He frequented cock fights, he drank deep at taverns, he was famous at rackets, and

he was prominent in many a midnight brawl.
No man was better known all the city over;
and his vices were forgiven for sake of his
virtues by a people who loved a spice of devilry
when tempered by liberality, humour, and
courtesy.

Even when he lay upon his death-bed his
fondness for joking did not desert him; the
world had been a mirthful place to him, and
mirthful he would remain till the curtain fell
upon him and darkness came. So when he
received from his neighbour, the Reverend John
Madden, Vicar of St. Anne's and Dean of
Kilmore, a letter severely reminding him of his
past, the particular offences of which, such as
profligacy, gaming, rioting, and blaspheming,
were in duty not omitted, and exhorting him
to repentance whilst time remained, his lordship
read the missive attentively and smiled archly.
Then he directed that this missive, which came
to him under cover, should be folded in another
paper, sealed, and directed to the Earl of
Kildare, to whom the Dean's messenger should
be directed to deliver it, he receiving two
guineas for his trouble.

Now my Lord Kildare was a puny, nervous little man, delicate, precise, religious, and effeminate. When he had married Lady Mary O'Brien, " one of the most shining beauties in the world, he would not take his wedding gloves off to embrace her " ; from which fact may an estimate of his character be formed. When therefore he read this letter charging him with so many vices he was well nigh choked with indignation. First he ran to my lady, and telling her Dean Madden had lost his senses, he showed her the letter to prove his word. Her ladyship read the epistle, grieving perhaps that its contents were not true, and then, observing that it was not written in the style of a madman, advised that it should be shown to the Archbishop of Dublin, Dr. John Hoadley.

On the spur of the moment his little lordship ordered his coach and drove to the episcopal palace, where he was lucky enough to find his Grace at home and ready to receive him. " Pray, your Grace," says he indignantly enough, "did you ever hear I was a profligate, a gamester, a blasphemer, a rioter, and in fact everything that's base and infamous ? "

"You, my lord," answered the Archbishop. "Everyone knows you are the pattern of humility, godliness, and virtue."

"True," cried his lordship. "But will you tell me what satisfaction can I have of a learned divine who under his own hand lays such vices to my charge?"

"Surely," his Grace replied, "no man in his senses that knows your lordship would presume to do so; and if any clergyman has been guilty of such an offence, your lordship will have ample satisfaction from the Spiritual Court."

Upon that my Lord Kildare showed his Grace the letter he had received from the Dean's servant, which both recognized to be written in that clergyman's hand. Fired with displeasure the Archbishop sent for the Dean, who in a short time presented himself; but before he entered the room his Grace begged Lord Kildare to walk into another apartment whilst he discoursed with the offending clergyman, which his lordship accordingly did.

When the Dean appeared he was handed the letter by his Grace, who sternly demanded if indeed he had written it.

" I did, your Grace," replied Dr. Madden.

" Mr. Dean," said the Archbishop, " I always thought you a man of sense and prudence, but this unguarded action must lessen you in the esteem of all good men; to throw out so many causeless invectives against the most unblemished nobleman in Europe, and accuse him of crimes to which he and his family have ever been strangers, must certainly be the effect of a distempered brain ; besides, sir, you have by this means laid yourself open to a prosecution in the ecclesiastical court, which will either oblige you publicly to recant what you have said or give up your possessions in the Church."

"Your Grace," the poor Dean answered, " I never either think, act, or write anything for which I am afraid to be called to an account before any tribunal upon earth ; and if I am to be prosecuted for discharging my duties, I will suffer patiently the severest penalties in justification for it," and, bowing, he retired without more ado.

My little lord, still hot with passion, drove home in his big coach and sent for a proctor of the Spiritual Court, to whom he committed the Dean's letter, ordering a citation to be sent to him without delay. In the meantime his Grace, who knew that the Dean, after the manner of his kind, had a large family to provide for, foresaw that ruin must attend him if prosecuted by so powerful a personage. Therefore filled with charitable intent, the Archbishop called at the Deanery and besought Dr. Madden to beg his lordship's pardon before the matter became public.

" Ask his pardon ? " exclaimed the Dean. " Why the man is dead."

" What, Lord Kildare dead ? " said his Grace, in horror.

" No, Lord Rosse," replied the Dean, whereon satisfactory explanations followed.

CHAPTER IV.

The management of Aungier Street Theatre—Rivalry of
the Rainsford Street house—Smock Alley rebuilt—
"The Tragedy of King Charles I."—Peg Woffington dances—Playing Ophelia—The celebrated Mr.
Quin—The romance of his birth—Taking to the
boards—Visit to Dublin—A terrible winter—Kitty
Clive's first appearance in the Irish capital—A
brilliant season.

IT will be remembered that Aungier Street
Theatre was built by " noblemen and gentlemen
of the first rank and consequence in the
nation." To them it now seemed desirable
they should superintend the concerns of the
stage, that its interests might be advanced,
and its prosperity placed on a firm basis. In
this they were "actuated by the noblest
motives," according to Hitchcock, who over-
looked the fact that in employing themselves
they found that delightful diversion which ever
arises from interfering with a business of which
nothing is known.

A committee was chosen from amongst them, a chairman appointed, and every Saturday they met to name the comedies and tragedies for performance during the week, to distribute the parts, and to settle a great variety of business. They also entertained laudable schemes for the future. The best actors were to be engaged, plays of merit were to be introduced, the wardrobe was to be enriched, and new scenery to be painted, fitted to the representations. Finally, all profits, instead of filling the purses of private individuals, were to be devoted to the public service.

Acting under this committee were the former managers of Smock Alley Theatre, an incompetent trio in themselves, whilst the general management was superintended by " a gentleman of character and fortune," named Swan, who in a moment of inflated vanity had been led to play Othello, and henceforth considered himself an actor of talent and an authority on stagecraft. It was not in the order of human affairs that so mixed a management could secure harmony or prosperity for any length of time. No novelty of any worth was forthcoming to amuse or amaze the town; the company engaged had little merit, but a matter of more consequence which helped to wreck the high hopes at first entertained, was that the theatre, built at a prodigious cost, was badly constructed, so that it required uncommon powers of voice to fill the house, and a great number of those in the gallery could neither see what took place on the stage nor hear the players' speeches, a fact that wrought much discontent and discord.

Meanwhile, the company at Rainsford Street Theatre continued to play for about a year with tolerable success; but when Henry VII. was produced at Aungier Street with a coronation scene which was declared the grandest sight the stage had yet exhibited, the town flocked to the latter theatre leaving the Rainsford Street players to posture before empty benches. In consequence their spirits were much cast down, but their inventive faculties were sharpened, and in a brief time they put on their boards a play called The Royal Merchant, or the Beggar's Bush, which had a burlesque procession named The Beggar's Coronation. This was so whimsical, so audacious, and so merry withal, that the fickle fancy of the town was greatly drawn to it, and success flowed in upon the players in so rapid a torrent as " to swell their pockets till they overflowed their banks, and watered the fields of many a publican. Debts were cleared, and every single person might, fearless, look at the dial on the tholsel " without expectancy of the bailiff's clutch. When this novelty ended, the houses became thin again, and after a three years' struggle the Rainsford Street playhouse was closed.

Before this event took place, a third theatre had opened its doors to the Dublin public. After deliberating some time the proprietors of the old playhouse in Smock Alley resolved to try their fortunes once more. Their theatre was conveniently situated, it had ancient and honourable traditions, and it was possible that if rebuilt it might again gain the popularity it had once commanded. Speculation in theatrical affairs had then, as now, its peculiar fascination. The proprietors needing funds, readily secured shareholders, the disused building was razed, and the foundation of the new house

laid on Monday, May 19th, 1735, with a pomp
and state equal to that which had marked a like
ceremony in Aungier Street.

In less than seven months from the laying
of its foundation stone, the theatre was built
and opened under the management of Lewis
Duval, to whom the Lord Mayor had granted
a license. The first performance took place on
December 11th, 1735, when the favourite
comedy of Love Makes a Man, and The
Fop's Fortune were played. So eager indeed
were the managers to open their theatre, that
"they began to play before the back of the
house was tiled in, which the town knowing,
they had not half an audience the first night,
but mended leisurely by degrees." The company engaged were chiefly those already
familiar to the town.

Hitchcock tells us the companies of Smock
Alley and Aungier Street "continued through
the season without any material occurrence,
with little profit to themselves or pleasure to
the town." In the summer they sought the
patronage of provincial audiences, one going
north, the other south, to enter into rivalry

84

once more on their return to Dublin in the autumn. In this contest Smock Alley theatre seems to have been the more successful, its chief attraction this season being the production of The Tragedy of King Charles the First.

This play, which excited the warmest admiration, was written by William Havard, a native of Dublin, who was "designed for the profession of a surgeon, but the stage displayed such charms, and made such an impression on his juvenile mind, that early in life he relinquished all other pursuits, and before the age of twenty had performed several characters at Smock Alley Theatre with applause." Fired by ambition, he went to London before he reached his majority and offered his services as a player to Giffard, manager of Goodman's Fields Theatre, who, esteeming him as "a person of some genius, and of a decent and sensible behaviour," engaged him at a low salary. Whilst there he wrote a tragedy called Scanderberg, which having only a tolerable share of merit, its want of success did not prompt him to further efforts just then.

Later, however, when Giffard became straitened in circumstances, he suggested that

Havard should write him another play. To this the youth consented, and selected as his theme the life and death of King Charles of martyred memory. But consent and performance were things apart with Havard, whose disposition was indolent and whose habit was postponement, as was well known to Giffard, who, that he might combat the indolence and uncertainty of genius, clapped Havard under lock and key and kept him there till he had completed his work.

The tragedy gained great applause, and its London success prepared the way for a favourable reception in Dublin, where it was performed to crowded houses. "Peculiarly happy in the choice of his subject," writes Hitchcock, "it was impossible even for moderate abilities not to work up such interesting events to some advantage. Mr. Havard had much merit in this respect. Few possessed of the least spark of sensibility can read the historian's relation of the unfortunate prince's taking his last leave of his children without the utmost emotion. On the stage its effect was prodigious. And my own observation can justify Mr. Davies's remark, that never were tears so plentifully shed as at the mournful separation of Charles and the young princes."

The while the Theatre Royal in Aungier Street was keeping up a brave spirit and attracting fair audiences by the dancing between the acts of Monsieur Boreau, William Delemain, and Peg Woffington. The latter had grown a young woman of uncommon attractions, whose bright grey eyes were full of witchery, whose mobile face was capable of the most varied expression, whose figure exhibited a grace and suppleness delightful to behold.

For years, however, she had remained a dancer, and it was only in February, 1737, that she was given her first speaking part, when she played Ophelia. News of her forthcoming appearance filled the town with excitement, for Peg Woffington was a neighbour's child, the daughter of " a widow woman " who earned her bread hard enough anyway, as a laundress. Sure the child herself had been known to the frequenters of the playhouse as an orange-seller, before she became a member of Madame Violante's troop ; and if her sweet singing and attractive ways did not win the hearts of the public, " leave it till again." Now that she was to take a decided step upward in a career which was full of promise, now that she was to play tragedy, it behoved all who knew her to lend their countenance and give her their ap- ʼ plause. And this they did with hearty good will. On the night in question the house, which was in the shape of a horse shoe, was thronged ; the first circle being appropriated to boxes, the price for which was five shillings and fivepence, where men and women of rank and quality, always in full dress, took their seats ; the upper boxes, for which two and twopence was charged, and the pigeon-holes or slips behind them, the price of which was thirteen pence, were occupied by the citizens with their wives and daughters ; the pit, admission to which cost three and three-pence, held the critics, lawyers, doctors, and the students from Trinity; whilst the sixpenny gallery was taken possession of by a droll and noisy company who relished a good play as well as their betters. Tallow candles stuck into circular iron sconces hung above the stage, and were now and then snuffed by the players in the pauses of tragic soliloquies, whilst the audience refreshed itself between the acts with oranges and nonpareils.

Like many another since and before her time, Peg Woffington began her career by mistaking its course : it was for comedy rather than tragedy that nature fitted her, as she was soon to find ; but meanwhile, by that personal experience which alone teaches, she had to discover the limits of her capacities and the bent of her talents. During the season that followed she began, as Hitchcock states, " to unveil those beauties and display those graces which for so many years afterwards charmed mankind." Her Lucy in The Virgin Unmasked drew houses, but never was she seen to greater advantage than when she played the parts of gallants and portrayed the dainty coxcombry of the male sex. The first appearance in what was called a breeches part was when she appeared as Phillis in The Conscious Lovers, and as a Female Officer in a farce of that name.

Much later, in April, 1739, she essayed for the first time the character of Sir Harry Wildair in The Constant Couple, a young spark, gay in disposition, liberal in character, loving adventure, frolicsome, rich and happy. This part had been a favourite with Robert Wilkes, amongst other famous players, and was associated with traditions of action, with memories of triumphs, so that Peg Woffington's attempt was regarded as daring by many, and as interesting by all. The night came · when she appeared as Sir Harry, before a crowded and critical audience, when, "so infinitely did she surpass expectation, that the applause she received was beyond any at that time ever known," says Hitchcock, who adds, "It was reserved for Miss Woffington to exhibit this elegant portrait of the young man of fashion in a style perhaps beyond the author's warmest ideas. Her Sir Harry Wildair was the subject of conversation in every polite circle and fixed her reputation as an actress. It was repeated upwards of twenty nights the first season, and never failed of drawing a most brilliant and numerous audience."

Two months later an event occurred which stirred the town to fresh interest. This was the appearance at Smock Alley Theatre of the celebrated Mr. Quin, then in the zenith of his glory.

Though born in London, on February 24th, 1693, James Quin was Irish by descent, his father being a Hibernian barrister who had entered himself at Lincoln's Inn, but who on inheriting a plentiful estate in his native country settled there, carrying with him his young son, the future actor. That the lad failed to inherit his father's property arose from the dealings of a malignant fate which had something of romance in its workings. The Hibernian barrister had married a seductive widow whose husband had some seven years previously sailed for the West Indies, where he trafficked in business ; and as meanwhile he neither wrote nor sent information of himself to his wife, she sought to console herself for the absence of him she believed dead by espousing one whom she loved. But before many years passed her peace was disturbed by the return of her husband, who was selfish enough to claim his wife. In this way James Quin, the offspring of her second union, was declared by the law illegitimate, and his prospects seemingly spoiled. What education he received was given him in Dublin, but this was not overmuch ; so that in after life it was asserted " he was deficient in literature," and it was true he laughed at those who read books by way of acquiring knowledge, saying in his assertive way that he preferred to read men, and that the world was the best book to understand.

By reason of his visits to Smock Alley Theatre he became struck by the stage and resolved to earn his bread by becoming a player. He therefore about the year 1714 applied for an engagement as an actor and was given small parts to perform. He had not been more than a year at Smock Alley when he was advised by Chetwood not to smother his rising genius in that kingdom, but to repair to London, there to try his fortune. Acting on which advice, he was soon enrolled amongst the Drury Lane company of players. By what men called accident, he soon stepped into notoriety ; for one night Mills, who was playing the important part of Bajazet in Tamerlane, was suddenly taken ill, when with much persuasion Quin was prevailed upon to read the part, which was thought a great undertaking for an actor of his standing. He succeeded so well that the audience applauded him through the whole course of the part; and on making himself perfect the next night, he performed the character " with redoubled applauses of approbation, and was complimented by several persons of distinction and dramatic taste upon his rising genius."

He now naturally expected that he would be advanced to play other parts of importance, but in this he was disappointed, and considering himself injured, he hired himself at the Lincoln's Inn Fields Theatre in 1717, where he remained for seventeen years, and by just degrees attained the highest round of perfection.

Meanwhile an event occurred in Quin's life which brought his name in a particular manner before the town. For it happened one afternoon between four and five of the clock, Quin was drinking a glass of wine at the Fleece tavern in Cornhill, with William Bowen, an actor born in Ireland who was fiery to a fault and passionate in his prejudices. Their conversation dwelt on the playhouse, as was natural and in a jocular manner Bowen reflected on Quin, saying he had acted Bajazet in a loose sort of manner. Quin thought Bowen had no occasion to value himself on his performances. By quick transition they fell into discourse about honesty, when mutual freedoms were taken on both sides, though they seemed to rise no higher than to cause a ruffled temper on either.

Then hastily Bowen rose up, flung down some money for the reckoning, saying he could not bear such abuse and would stay no longer in the company. He had not been gone a quarter of an hour when there came a porter to the tavern first asking for Mr. Bowen, and then inquiring if Mr. Quin were not present, and when the latter went to him the fellow whispered in his ear. Quin quitted the Fleece, and six doors lower down he met Bowen, who said he desired to drink a pint of wine with him, upon which Quin urged him to return to the Fleece, but he refusing, they went to the Pope's Head tavern, where being shown into a room and calling for wine, they sat down. Quin desired his companion might state what he had to say, when the latter declared he had been injured past verbal reparation, and nothing but fighting should make him amends. Quin endeavoured to persuade him to sleep upon his quarrel, and then if he could not come into temper next day he would ask his pardon in the same company as he had injured him ; but Bowen bade him not trifle with him, saying he would now do himself justice, and drawing his sword, in a violent passion swore he would run Quin through the body if he did not draw in his own defence.

Then came a flash and clash of swords, when one weapon dropped to the ground, and blood spurted from Bowen, who took his antagonist by the hand, kissed him, bade him take his hat and wig and go back to the Fleece, and afterwards to make his escape. Bowen was conveyed to his home in a chair, and three days later he died. Quin did not seek to escape, but was indicted and tried for murder on the 17th of April, 1718, when he pleaded he had done nothing but that to which he had been compelled, and that had he not opposed Bowen's violence he must have courted self-murder.

He was found guilty of manslaughter. The punishment meted out to him was slight, for in the autumn of the year he was playing as usual and drawing good houses to Lincoln's Inn Fields Theatre. From here he went to Covent Garden, December 7th, 1732, and subsequently to Drury Lane in the beginning of the season 1734.

The first actor on the stage at this time, his high estimate of himself was generally accepted by others. Heavy in figure, coarse in feature, he was somewhat pompous in manner and not invariably free from affectation when he desired to impress. The pleasures of life he appreciated to an uncommon degree, and to sit at the tables of the great, where he ate turtle and venison and drank rare wines, was a source of satisfaction on which he was wont to dwell. Though frequently bad-tempered he was essentially good-natured, and as a narrator of humorous stories he certainly excelled.

His Irish origin, the romantic story of his parentage, his reputation as an actor and as the successful combatant in a duel, won him a regard which was almost affection from the people,

who now eagerly flocked to hear him declaim
long speeches as Cato and Juba, and to see
him in such comedy parts as Sir John Brute
and Heartfree. And such was his reputation,
that when at the end of the season he took his
benefit, the results were a hundred and twenty-
six pounds, " at that time esteemed a great
sum."

In the autumn of 1739 he returned to London,
and the winter which followed was so severe as
to gravely interfere with all theatrical enterprise
in Dublin. This memorable season began with
a most violent storm of wind which worked a
prodigious deal of damage not only at sea and
in the harbour, but likewise inland. Then
from the 29th of December until the 8th of
February, 1740, came a terrible frost which
froze the Liffey so that people walked in
numbers on the ice, until such time as the Corporation employed men to cut a passage through
it that boats might carry coals to the city, which
were sold at an exorbitant price. The House
of Commons met on the 25th of January, but
adjourned on account of the terrible cold; at
the Deer Park a number of miserable men and

women met to cut down trees for firing, and were only prevented from their purpose by the calling out of the Dragoon Guards, who seized upon fourteen persons and drove away the rest. Snow lay for weeks several feet deep in the streets; vast numbers were frozen to death; his Grace the Duke of Devonshire gave a hundred pounds for the relief of the poor; the Hon. Lady Betty Brownlowe gave four times that sum; the Hon. William Conolly ordered one hundred and thirty sacks of meal and corn to be distributed amongst the distressed, and other kind-hearted Christians followed this example of charity; whilst Lords Mountjoy and Tullamore, Sir Thomas Pendergast, and Alderman Pearson, went about the city in person collecting money for the starving population.

Aungier Street Theatre appears to have shut its doors from the beginning of this terrible period, but Smock Alley kept open for a while, and in the Dublin *Evening Post* we read that its manager, Duval, " has erected in the pit (which he designs to continue during the frost) a fire engine in which is kept a large fire burning the whole time of the performance, and warmed the house in such a manner as gave great satisfaction to the audience." But even this device on his part failed to attract playgoers, and soon he was obliged to close his theatre.

Both houses opened again in April, on the 29th of which month Peg Woffington played Lappet in The Miser, at the Aungier Street house; and on May 1st, Silvia, and on the 12th of that month, Polly in the Beggar's Opera, after which the theatre seems to have closed for the season. The severe winter and the famine that followed left the people little spirit for enjoyment, so that all theatrical enterprise was at its lowest ebb in Ireland. We are told by Genest, who says it is scarcely credible, though strictly true, that one of the players, Dyer, had a salary of merely eight shillings a week, Isaac Sparks had twelve shillings, Elrington received a guinea, and the rest in proportion. Occasionally it happened that but the half of these salaries were received by the actors, whilst, again, not a penny was paid them. On unquestionable authority, it is stated by Genest that the acting managers were " so reduced in their finances and so exhausted in their credit, that they were once obliged to repair to the theatre on the evening of a play dinnerless; the first shilling that came into the house they dispatched for a loin of mutton, the second for bread, the third for liquor, and so on until they had satisfied the demands of nature."

To remedy this depressed condition of affairs, the managers of Aungier Street Theatre resolved not only to engage Quin and Ryan, already popular favourites in Ireland, but likewise Kitty Clive, the first actress in her own line, and Mademoiselle Chateauneuf, then esteemed the best female dancer in Europe. These four entertainers were brought over from London in June, 1741, when never in the history of the Irish stage had so brilliant a season been known.

The appearance of Kitty Clive in Dublin was certain to meet with success; for not only was she a delightful, vivacious, and accomplished actress, but she was likewise the daughter of a gallant Irishman, one William Raftor, who had rashly joined the cause of King James, fought for him at the Battle of the Boyne, and followed his fallen fortunes into France.

This conduct of William Raftor had involved the forfeiture of his good estate, which was handed over to the adherents of William of Orange. Raftor received a captain's commission from Louis XIV., who showed him much favour; but after some years of foreign service, this soldier desired to return to England, which he did after having received pardon from Queen Anne, who was disposed to look kindly on those who had fought and suffered for her brother's sake.

A man with a martial figure, a record for bravery, and a history not unacquainted with romance, he soon wooed and won a widow rich and young, who bore him many children, amongst whom was the sprightly, witty Catherine, who was born in the year 1711, and eventually became known to fame as Kitty Clive.

She who had jumped and crowed in her mother's arms as if greeting the joys of life; she who had sung and danced in the nursery to gain applause of the wondering world of childhood around, looked forward to the wider subjugation of a maturer audience, from the time she had entered her teens. Here was that shaping of an intent towards the gaining of a reality ; that foreshadowing of fate mistaken for free choice. With her seventeenth year came the event of chiefest import in her life, when one day she stood eager and trembling, with all the nervousness and self-confidence of her age, an aspirant for stage honours, ready to sing and to recite, and anxious to gain the admiration and approval of the great Colley Cibber, an execrable poet-laureate, a writer of excellent comedies, an accomplished actor, and the manager of Drury Lane Theatre. The result of this interview was her engagement as a player at a salary of twenty shillings a week.

Her first appearance was as a page in a cap and feather, a page that burst into song in and out of season. Her voice was sweet, her manner winning, and she gained extraordinary applause. From that time forward the path seemed fair before this lucky mortal. She pleased her manager, she delighted the town, she had saved a play that had been perilously near damnation, and she had been called by a pretty fellow in a stage box, "a charming little devil."

In her representations of singing chamber-maids roguish and fascinating, of innocent country girls wilful and witching, of widows mirthful and enticing, of viragoes sharp-tongued and witty—those stock characters in the comedies of the eighteenth century—she espe-cially excelled; her melodious voice, sprightly action, and merry face furnishing admirable supports to such parts. When about nineteen she married a brother of Mr. Baron Clive, but if domestic happiness ever existed for her, its duration was brief. Husband and wife parted by mutual consent; but though living in an age when licentiousness was rife, and belonging to a profession which scandal assailed, her reputation remained unstained, and she was, as Henry Fielding has expressed it, "the best daughter, the best sister, and the best friend" imaginable.

Not only did her circle number Henry Field-ing, and George Farquhar, but amongst other famous men it included Horace Walpole, Oliver Goldsmith, and Dr. Johnson. "Clive, sir," the latter would say, " is a good thing to sit by ; she always understands what you say "; and not to be outdone in courtesy, Kitty would smile archly at the ponderous philosopher and remark : " I love to sit by Dr. Johnson, he always entertains me." At times her temper was quick, her tongue sharp, and she was wont to exchange violent passages at arms with her fellow-players, with Quin, amongst the rest, whom she called her " great bear," and later, with Garrick, whom she spoke of as " little Davy," but her gusts of passion soon blew over, and she delighted in remaining good friends with all.

She was in the meridian of her powers and in the full flavour of her fame when she appeared at Aungier Street Theatre, to which, with Quin and Ryan, she drew large and fashionable audiences. It was during this season that The Masque of Comus was acted for the first time in Ireland, Quin speaking the part of Comus, Mrs. Clive representing Euphrosyne, whilst the other characters " were disposed of with great care and propriety." Duburg, a man of much talent, had prepared the music, the band was led by Pasquilino, and the chief dancers were Mademoiselle Chateauneuf and Monsieur Laluze, and the whole performance was pronounced the best entertainment presented to the town for many years.

Kitty Clive and Ryan returned to London at the close of the summer season, but Quin went with the Aungier Street company to Cork and Limerick, returning with them in October, when he once more entertained a Dublin audience, to their delight : but a greater novelty and a finer pleasure were in store for them, for in the December of this year the famous Mrs. Cibber made her first appearance in Ireland in the Aungier Street Theatre.

CHAPTER V.

The homes of the Irish nobility—Love of entertainment
—The Castle balls—The Duke of Dorset as Lord
Lieutenant—Miss Wesley's dancing—Receptions at
Bishop Clayton's—Concerts and Ridottos—Miss
Letitia Pilkington—Dancing the order of the day—
That dear Dean Swift—Miss Constantina Grierson.

THE theatre was not the only place where
acting could be witnessed, for so great was the
delight taken by the nobility in this form of
entertainment, that plays performed by amateurs
of high rank were frequently given at the Castle
and in the drawing-rooms of the aristocracy.
They were, however, but one of various kinds
of diversion enjoyed by men and women of
quality, whose families to the number of between
four and five thousand had at this time resi-
dences in Dublin.

For in days before the legislative union
despoiled the country of its independence and
the capital of its prosperity, the latter was
remarkable for its gaiety and brilliancy. Not

106

less splendid than that of St. James's was
the Viceregal Court, where frequent levées
were held, attended by women whose beauty
was the admiration of all lands, the choicest
wealth of its own, and by men whose bravery
won them world-wide renown; the wit of
the one sex and the gallantry of the other
making them themes for a thousand tales.

The houses of the nobility were palatial
mansions built of white granite from the
Wicklow Mountains, and decorated interiorly
by artists summoned from abroad. Furnished
with the greatest magnificence, and filled by an
army of menials, they were by day scenes of
open-hearted hospitality where, gathered round
sumptuously supplied tables, were crowds of
guests, which no matter how numerous did not
hold one too many; whilst night after night
they were lighted by a blaze of tapers, and
thronged by those whose joyous feet fell light
as snowflakes upon spacious wax-surfaced
floors to the hilarious sounds of fiddles and
flutes.

Whilst Lord Carteret was Viceroy, from 1724
to 1731, scarce a week passed during his

residence at the Castle that he did not give a ball
there. His successor, Lionel, Duke of Dorset,
though not less fond of pleasure did not entertain
with such frequency. However, the assemblies
over which he and his Duchess presided were
marked by magnificence. In a letter written
by his Excellency in November, 1731, to Lady
Suffolk, he tells her of the finery seen at the
Castle on his birthday. " I believe," he says,
more rich cloaths were never seen together,
except at St. James's, and some of them so
well chose that one would have sworn a certain
countess of my acquaintance had given her
assistance upon this occasion.

" I should not do justice to Capt. Pearce's
genius if I did not give you some account of
the ball room that we fitted up for the night's
entertainment, the usual place was thought too
little, and therefore it was resolved to make use
of the old hall, which had been long disused
and very much out of repair; however, he so
contriv'd it that I never saw a more beautiful
scene. I am sure you won't think that an im-
proper expression when I tell you the walls
were all covered with canvas painted in per-

spective, the space was a large one, but it was so contriv'd of to make it look as big again ; there were your Arches, your Pyramids, your Obelisks, and Pillars of all orders and denominations; in short, there were all those things that your fine folk talk on nowadays ; and the lights were so perfectly well disposed that, upon my word, it had a most surprising fine effect.

" Some jokers were of opinion that our room might be better than our company, but they were perfectly convinced to the contrary when they saw how it was filled."

One of that gay company, Mrs. Pendavers, a handsome young widow of thirty summers, who afterwards became Mrs. Delany, wrote to her sister describing the entertainment. The room where the ball was held was made as light as a summer's day. " I never," says she, "saw more company in one place ; abundance of finery, and indeed many very pretty women. There were two rooms for dancing. The whole apartment of the Castle was open, which consists of several very good rooms ; in one there was a supper, where everybody went at what hour they liked best, and vast profusion of meat and drink,

which you may be sure gained the hearts of all
guzzlers. The Duke and Duchess broke
through their reserved way and were very
obliging; indeed, it was very handsome the
whole entertainment, but attended with great
crowding and confusion."

The handsome young widow who wrote this
account was dressed on the occasion in blue
and white satin that she had brought from
England, and "a new laced head"; whilst the
friend who accompanied her was decked in
green satin embroidered finely in green and
silver. The Duchess of Dorset was habited in
Irish poplin, which she mightily wished to bring
into fashion; and Miss Wesley, who performed
miracles by her dancing, adorned her gown of
simple white satin. "You may imagine," says
Mrs. Delany, the name she best is known by,
"such a little pretty creature does not want for
praises: were I her mother, I should not expose
her to so *many;* she is of an age to be spoiled
by them, unless she has an uncommon share of
sense." Again Mrs. Delany describes a ball
given at the Castle in honour of the King's
coronation, where everything was "decently

ordered, and French dancing in abundance."
Of course there was a vast assemblage of people
all bent on enjoyment, and when supper was
announced everything was found prepared with
great magnificence—three large tables besides
the Duke's, covered with all sorts of provisions
very well disposed. "After that they went to
dancing again : it was so hot and crowded that
our courage would hold out but for half a dance.
Between twelve and one we came home, and
were very well pleased to lay us down." Mrs.
Delany, then visiting Ireland for the first time
saw with unaccustomed eyes the social life of
the capital, which she fluently describes. Her
stay was made with Dr. Clayton, Bishop of
Killaloe, and his wife, who lived in a stately
mansion resembling Devonshire House, and
standing in Stephen's Green. "The apartments
are handsome," Mrs. Delany writes, "and
furnished with gold-coloured damask, virtues,
and busts, and pictures that the Bishop brought
with him from Italy. A universal cheerful-
ness reigns in the house. They keep a very
handsome table: six dishes of meat are constantly at dinner, and six plates at supper."

The Bishop was a man of commanding deportment, who "united the dignity of an ecclesiastic with the ease of a fine gentleman." His better qualities were "tarnished by obsequious ambition"; he lived freely, and his religious views were wide; but this latter was a fact he judiciously concealed in his ecclesiastical breast until he had been made a spiritual peer. His wife was the daughter of Lord Chief Justice Donnellan, a stately woman who loved the world not less than her lord. Both were extremely hospitable, their hearts "being answerable to their fortunes," and were universally popular. On Wednesday nights Mrs. Clayton received abundance of good and agreeable company in her rooms wainscoted with oak, the panels, the high chimney all carved, the ceiling stuccoed, looking-glasses and portraits well disposed upon the walls, the furniture done in yellow damask and the floors covered with the finest Persian carpet that ever was seen.

After the hostess had made her compliments to her friends, she sat at the commerce table, those who did not play being entertained with music, Mrs. Delany seating herself at the harpsichord, when she received great honours for her performance on that instrument. These parties, which began at seven, ended by half-past ten, when chairs were called for, and coaches conveyed the guests home amidst great bustle and courteous expressions of the gratification all had received.

The generality of the people she met pleased this visitor well, for they " all behave themselves very decently according to their rank ; now and then an oddity breaks out, but none so extra-ordinary but that I can match them in England. There is a heartiness amongst them that is more *like Cornwall* that any I have known, and great sociableness."

Concerning this latter-mentioned trait she frequently speaks ; indeed in her letters there is continual mention of dances and balls and other parties of pleasure, until in reading those almost forgotten pages, one can hear the fiddle's lusty scrape and see the quaintly-dressed figures move athwart the wax-lit scenes as vividly as if they who danced had not returned to dust.

For instance, Lord Mountjoy, a gracious and

sweet-spoken man, gave a ball, mighty select and limited to twenty-four couple, who were only admitted by ticket, and were bidden for seven by the clock. The Duke and Duchess of Dorset came with their youngest daughter, amongst a brilliant company that were mostly titled. As they entered they were served with tea and coffee; then the music struck up merrily enough, when every lad handed out his lass whose turn it was to dance, for only twelve took the floor at a time, and when they had danced twice, the other twelve took their place. The Duchess did not join in this gaiety because she had a headache; nor did Mrs. Clayton, as such would be beneath the dignity of a bishop's wife ; but the rest enjoyed it mightily. Then when the clock struck eleven their Graces went upstairs, when all sorts of cold meats, fruits, sweetmeats, and wines were served ; they being followed by those who were not at the moment dancing ; the others taking their turn when room was made for them. Then dancing began again and was kept up till four in the morning, amidst laughter and abundance of good spirits.

Occasionally there were fine reviews in the Phœnix Park, " which is far beyond St. James's or Hyde Park " ; the Duchess of Dorset in great state surrounded by the *beau monde ;* the bishop's wife in a gorgeous equipage which, if it did not exceed her Grace's in splendour, was finer than all others ; " but in every respect Mrs. Clayton outshines her neighbours, not that that is easily done here, for people understand not only living well, but politely."

Concerts and ridottos were also attended, and on the feast of St. Cecilia fine music, which began at ten and ended at four, was given at St. Patrick's Church, which was filled by a great concourse of people. And visits of ceremony were paid to such personages as Dr. Vanlewin and his cheerful and sensible family, when the time was passed by all present admitting what was the quality on which they valued themselves most, and afterwards what they most disliked in their characters. This clever physician is best remembered as the father of Letitia Pilkington, who was considered a wit and a genius. She was, moreover, a friend of Dean Swift, and formed one of the female *coterie* in whose company he found pleasure.

She had on one occasion sent him verses on his birthday, and was later introduced to him by a lady of whom he inquired if Letitia were her daughter. When told that she was Mrs. Pilkington, he said, " What, that poor little child married ? God help her, she is early inured to trouble " ; which was a sad truth, for her husband, a parson, was a worthless fellow. The Dean at once became interested in her, and engaged Pilkington to preach for him at St. Patrick's Church the following Sunday, when Swift went through the service without once looking at the prayer-book. After church a vast number of poor people gathered round him, as was their custom, when he gave to all save one, an old woman with dirty hands ; and her he refused, saying that though she was a beggar, water was not so scarce but that she might wash. That night he asked the Pilkingtons to sup with him and entertained them with his wit ; afterwards he handed Letitia to her coach, slipping into her palm, as he did so, the exact sum she and her husband had given at the offertory that morning, together with the cost of her coach hire.

One who was famed for her pleasant assemblies was the Hon. Mrs. Butler, a prominent figure of whom much more, later. At one of her gatherings mentioned by Mrs. Delany, she began her entertainment with commerce, and basset, and cards of all sorts. When this was over at ten o'clock, little tables were placed before the company as they sat, containing plates with various kinds of cold meats neatly cut, and sweetmeats wet and dry, sago, jellies, chocolate and salvers of wine. As they were eating and enjoying themselves, the hostess suddenly bethought of sending for fiddlers, and no sooner had they arrived than up sprang the young people, and in the twinkling of an eye, eight couple of the cleverest dancers ever beheld were on the floor, and were in no hurry to leave off, for 'twas near to three in the morning before they dispersed.

Dancing indeed was the order of this happy day, unfretted by morbid introspection, inequality of sex, doubt, metaphysical criticisms, and despair. Amusement was grasped at, welcomed, and enjoyed at all times, and of all diversions dancing gave the chiefest joy, the brightest form of entertainment that could be offered to friend or guest.

One spring day with fitful gleams of sun in the bracing air, Mrs. Delany and a few friends drove out three miles beyond the town to visit Kit Usher, a sensible, plain, good-humoured man, married to a poor meek little woman who never made or marred sport. They reached their destination at two, when the best in his house was immediately at the disposal of the visitors, fowl, lamb, pigeon pie, Dutch beef, tongue, cockles, salad, " much variety of liquors and the finest syllabub that ever was tasted."

All having eaten heartily, Mrs. Delany was asked to give them some music, when she made the harpsichord jangle a little. The host then took down his fiddle, on which his little daughters set out to dance, he joining them, and finally the spirit seizing all present, they took the floor likewise, and away they went capering and dancing to their hearts' delight, never giving over their sport till long past one in the morning.

As may be supposed, Dean Swift was a prominent figure in Dublin society at this period, only a few years before his brilliant mind grew dark, before the tree began to wither at the top. Not only was his wit the delight of all polite circles, but his charity caused him to be worshipped by the poor, for half his income was devoted to decayed families, whilst he retained five hundred a year, "the first sum of that magnitude of which he was master," that he might lend it out to mechanics and labourers, giving them five pounds at a time, which they repaid by instalments of two shillings; in this way enabling the industrious and worthy to purchase tools and materials for their work.

In the true spirit of charity his donations to his humbler brethren were made at the cost of some little personal sacrifice; as when for instance, on leaving a fine party he ran home through the rain that he might give his coach fare to a beggar unable to walk; or when he deprived himself of a pint of wine that he might give its price to one who needed bread.

Mrs. Delany describes him as "a very odd

companion, if that expression is not too familiar for so extraordinary a genius ; he talks a great deal and does not require many answers ; he has infinite spirits, and says abundance of good things in his common way of discourse." A great many extraordinary tales were told of his humour, his satire, and his sense, but perhaps the most characteristic is that relating to the visits he paid Dr. Theophilus Bolter, when this time-serving divine was promoted to the Bishopric of Clonfert in 1722, to the see of Elphin two years later, and was made Archbishop of Cashel in 1729. When Bolter was first created a spiritual peer, the patriotic Dean called upon him and hoped he would use his influence in the Upper House in his country's service, whereon his lordship answered "his bishopric was very small, and he would never have a better if he did not oblige the court" ; to which Swift in his blunt way answered, "When you have a better, I hope you will become an honest man ; until then farewell."

Much the same reply was given by Bolter when he was raised to the see of Elphin, to a similar suggestion made by Swift ; but when the former was elevated to the Archbishopric, and the Dean called on him, his Grace said, "I well know that no Irishman will ever be made Primate, and as I can rise no higher in fortune or station, I will now zealously promote the good of my country."

A more whimsical story relates how the Dean went to dine with a farmer named Reilly, living near Quilca, when he found his hostess very fantastically dressed for the occasion, and her son decorated with a silver-laced hat. The Dean bowed low before her, treating her with the ceremony due to a duchess, and then proposed that the husband should show him over his demesne. "The devil a foot of land belongs to me or any of my line," says the farmer. "I have a pretty good lease from my Lord Fingall, but he will not renew it." Swift asked when he was to see Mrs. Reilly, on which the farmer in surprise replied, "There she is before you." The Dean stared and then answered, "Impossible. I always heard Mrs. Reilly was a prudent woman: she would never dress herself out in silks and ornaments only fit for ladies of fortune and fashion. Sure Mrs. Reilly would never wear anything beyond plain stuffs and other suitable things."

On this the hostess took the hint and disappeared, to return in apparel suitable to her station, whereon her guest went and took her hand and told her in a friendly and confidential way, "Your husband wanted to pass off a fine lady upon me dressed up in silk in the pink of the mode, for his wife, but I was not to be taken in."

He then cut the silver lace off her son's hat and put it in the fire, but presently took it out again, wrapped it in paper, and thrust it into his pocket. Then in great good-humour he entertained the farmer and his wife, ate heartily of the dinner, and in parting from them, said, " I don't intend to rob you of your son's hat lace. I have only changed its form for a better one. God bless you, and thanks for your good entertainment ; " saying which he handed them the paper, in which they found not only the lace, but four guineas.

At this time a number of learned ladies hovered round the poor man, of whom Mrs. Pilkington, who was something of an adventuress, made one. A more ingenious and gifted personage was Constantina Grierson, who was declared the most extraordinary woman her own or any other age produced, for she wrote Greek epigrams, gave proof of her knowledge of the Latin tongue by her dedication to Lord Carteret of an edition of Tacitus, and wrote many fine poems in English. She rose to eminence solely by continual study and the force of her genius, and her abilities were rewarded by the Lord Lieutenant obtaining for her husband a patent to be the King's printer, in which her life was inserted.

A third of these wits who was more interesting to Swift was Miss Kelly, whose beauty and good-humour was reported to have gained an entire conquest over his heart. Her father, Captain Dennis Kelly, who had a very good estate, was committed to the Tower in 1722 on suspicion of corresponding with the Pretender; whilst her uncle, the Rev. George Kelly, was charged with having treasonable correspondence with James Stuart, was tried by the House of Lords, and sentenced for life to imprisonment in the Tower, from which he escaped.

When Miss Kelly fell ill of a cold, she wrote to the Dean asking him what books he would recommend to improve her mind. He sent her some liquorice, and with it "a fable, very prettily applied, of Lycoris." The cold turned into a pleuratic disorder, when the Dean attended her bedside; "but his presence, though it cheered, did not heal her, and a few months later, in October, 1733, she died, being destroyed by the ignorance of an Irish physician, one Gorman."

In all circles, high and low, the playhouse and its doings were discussed as subjects of common and unfailing interest, and the engagement of an actor or actress unknown to the town was hailed with anticipatory pleasure, as was at this precise time the advent of Mrs. Cibber, whose beauty was greatly extolled, and whose talents were much debated by those who had seen her on the London stage.

CHAPTER VI.

Susanna Maria Cibber and her spouse—One Stint the
candle-snuffer—Mrs. Cibber's success in Dublin—
The famous Mr. Handel and his oratorios—
Woffington and Garrick at Smock Alley—
Enthusiasm of the town—Tom Sheridan's first
appearance—Quarrel with Theo Cibber—Old Trinity
—Town and Gown—The college boys take Sheridan's
part—Riot in the theatre.

SUSANNA MARIA CIBBER, who now appeared
before Dublin audiences, was a player who had
long occupied the attention of London town
and given it vast entertainment, not only by her
brilliant talents, but by certain episodes in her
career. The daughter of a decent upholsterer in
Covent Garden, the sister of Thomas Arne,
doctor of music, she had early in life delighted
all hearers by the quality of her voice. Her
figure was graceful, her face was winsome,
and her manner charmed to perfection.

Some ill fate induced her to marry Theophilus
Cibber, son of old Colley Cibber, perhaps the

worst poet laureate England has known. He was, however, an excellent actor, an ingenious playwriter, and a manager of ability. Theo Cibber had "a person far from pleasing, and the features of his face were rather disgusting." Though he was not without merit as a player, he preferred to live on the earnings of his wife than to profit by his own exertions ; and was, moreover, a scoundrel of the deepest dye.

In her desire to forsake the concert hall for the dramatic stage, Mrs. Cibber was encouraged by her husband, who foresaw more remuneration in the change. Her father-in-law accordingly instructed her in the art in which he excelled, and so apt was his pupil that on her appearance as Zara in the tragedy of that name, in 1736, she gave both surprise and delight to her audience by the justness and beauty of her performance.

Her career led upwards, her fame increased. But not satisfied with the amount he secured by her salary, her profligate husband sought other means of increasing his gains. He therefore made known to her "a romp and a good-natured boy": the individual so designated being a young gentleman of fortune named William

Sloper, whom Cibber introduced under the appropriate name of Mr. Benefit. In due time Susanna fell in love and eloped with Sloper to Burnham, from which place her husband, accompanied by a sergeant of the guards, took her by force and lodged her at the Bull Head Tavern, near Clare Market, under the care of one Stint, candle-snuffer to Covent Garden Theatre. Here her brother sought her with the intention of taking charge of her, but Stint would not admit him, whereon a sympathizing crowd broke into the house, beat the candle-snuffer sorely, tore the clothes from his back, and rescued the fair Susanna, who in this becomingly dramatic manner was restored to her lover.

The husband who had plotted her downfall posed as a man dishonoured, and sought consolation in the law courts. He estimated his loss at five thousand pounds, and was awarded ten. Whilst the scrimmage was proceeding Mrs. Cibber declined to appear on the London stage, but having received an offer from the Aungier Street manager, she accepted it on the agreement that she was to receive three hundred pounds for the season, a sum which Hitchcock states " they were well enabled to pay from the money she drew, though to her first night there was not ten pounds."

Her earliest appearance at the theatre was made on Saturday evening, December 21st, 1741, when she played Indiana in The Conscious Lovers. Before long she drew great houses, especially when she and Quin appeared in the same cast. Richard Cumberland, who witnessed their performance in The Fair Penitent, gives us a description of the entertainment which delighted our ancestors. He tells us that " Quin presented himself on the rising of the curtain in a green velvet coat embroidered down the seams, an enormous full-bottomed periwig, rolled stockings, and high-heeled square-toed shoes; with very little variation of cadence, and in a deep full tone, accompanied by a sawing kind of action which had more of the Senate than of the stage in it, he rolled out his heroics with an air of dignified indifference that seemed to disdain the plaudits that were bestowed upon him. Mrs. Cibber, in a key high pitched but sweet withal, sung, or rather recitatived, Rowe's harmonious strain, something in the manner of the improvisatories: it was so extremely wanting in contrast, though it did not wound the ear, it wearied it. When she had once recited two or three speeches, I could anticipate the manner of every succeeding one: it was like a long old legendary ballad of innumerable stanzas, every one of which is sung to the same tune, eternally chiming in the ear without variation or relief."

Whilst the Aungier Street Theatre was crowded, the Smock Alley house was empty. To remedy this unprofitable condition of affairs, Duval made every exertion, engaging one Wright, "an actor of great merit," to appear as Lear, the principal players who supported him being Mrs. Furnival, Isaac Sparks, Elrington, Morgan, and Wetherilt. Moreover, he engaged Chetwood, who for twenty years had been prompter at Drury Lane, to whose advice the Dublin stage owed many advantages ; amongst them being the working of the wings by means of a barrel underneath, which moved them together at the same time with the scenes; an innovation that was publicly boasted of as a masterpiece of mechanism.

But Smock Alley Theatre failed to prosper, for not only had the manager to contend against the attractions of James Quin and Susanna Cibber, but likewise did the new concert hall built in Fishamble Street divert public attention from his house. This had been opened on the 2nd of October, 1741, and the citizens, ever passionate lovers of music, had flocked eagerly to its concerts. Their delight was heightened when, some months later, "the famous Mr. Handel" gave his first oratorio here. Mrs. Cibber, who it will be remembered had early in life gained fame as a singer, took part in the oratorios, and Handel so highly approved of her voice that he altered one of the airs in the Messiah, the better to suit it.

Quin returned to London in February, 1742, but Mrs. Cibber remained and played Polly in The Beggar's Opera with great success. Quin being no longer in the field, and Mrs. Cibber's performances having lost their novelty, it occurred to Duval to woo fortune afresh. And for this purpose he played a trump card, in inviting to Smock Alley three such personages as Peg Woffington, Garrick, and Giffard.

On her appearance in London, Peggy had gained extraordinary applause, beyond any ever known at that time. Her talents were discussed in coffee houses and taverns, critics lauded her, women of quality flocked to her, the town was in love with her.

And already the fame of David Garrick, a young man of Irish descent, had travelled to Ireland, creating desire to witness the performances of this wine merchant who had dared to turn player, to the horror of his respectable family. Not twelve months previously, indeed, to be precise, on the 19th of October, 1741, he had made his first bow to a London audience at Giffard's playhouse in Goodman's Fields; but even in days when the press took small notice of the theatre, news reached Dublin that he had discarded rant and spoken his lines as might a man in real life, greatly to the scorn of such actors as Cibber and Quin; that he imitated nature, turned from convention, and marked out a new way for himself. Likewise had the rumour reached Dublin of the commendations he had received. How the most elegant company including great ministers, dukes and duchesses by the dozen, wits, critics, pamphleteers and poets, had flocked to the little playhouse in an unsavoury district to see this wonder of the age, this young gentleman who was about to revolutionize the stage.

Peg Woffington and David Garrick were engaged to appear in Dublin in June, July, and August, 1742. News of this enterprise caused immense excitement amongst a people to whom the concerns of the stage were of much importance. Every item of gossip regarding them was repeated and exaggerated; they were lovers for a fact; 'twas certain they would marry; sure what better match could either of them make? Aye, but Peggy herself was a winsome woman; wouldn't a glance of her eyes put the "come hither" on any man?

The Dublin *Mercury* of the 8th of June announced that they were hourly expected from England to entertain the nobility and gentry during the summer season. Crowds waited for hours on the quays to receive them, amongst them, the observed of all eyes, being Peggy's mother, a person of vast importance, mighty grand in the black velvet cloak which, as the town knew, her dutiful daughter had sent her all the way from London.

It was on the evening of the 15th of June, 1742, when Peg Woffington gave her famous personation of Sir Harry Wildair. Boxes had been engaged by the nobility weeks previously; the doors of the theatre were besieged by perspiring crowds hours before they opened; and the scramble which eventually took place for seats was beyond anything ever witnessed. Even for the time of year the weather was intensely warm, but the expectant audience sat good-humouredly awaiting her appearance, the gallery now and then greeting by friendly and witty remarks the arrivals of well-known personages as they entered pit or box, and furthermore diverting themselves by singing and badinage.

And when eventually this daughter of the people appeared before them, such a roar went up as made her heart beat and brought tears to her eyes, so that she could not recover herself for some time. When she did the fun began, and every witty speech, every coy movement of her head or witching expression of her eyes,

133

was emphasized by laughter that was wholesome to hear.

On the third night of the season Garrick appeared in an historical play called The Life and Death of King Richard the Third, he playing Richard, and Peg Woffington Lady Anne. Not only was every seat in the house occupied, but scores stood and hundreds were turned from the doors. And as the tragedy proceeded such applause was given as might be heard on the quays. Critical as well as enthusiastic, the audience saw the character of the King played as it had never been represented, seized upon Garrick's merits, and admitted his power.

And so pleased was he by their appreciation, so satisfied of their acumen, that he resolved to play before them, for the first time, the character of Hamlet. To the Dublin citizens of that day Shakespeare was a sacred name ; no matter how badly staged, how wretchedly acted, his plays were certain to draw houses packed with those whose innate sense of poetry made them appreciate the music of his words, whose sagacity fed upon the wisdom of his philosophy. That Garrick should first impersonate the melancholy Dane before them, was regarded as a compliment to their critical faculties. The highest expectations were formed of his representation, but they were not disappointed. Never had such a Hamlet been seen. His lines were beautifully spoken, his action appropriate, his appearance stately and full of a tender sadness that begot sympathy and earned love.

Throughout the three months of their engagement the enthusiasm caused by their performances never abated; nay, if possible it increased. Such indeed was its force that women continually went into hysterics over Ophelia's madness or Cordelia's wrongs, and shrieked at the combat of Hamlet or the death of Richard. The summer, as has already been remarked, being unusually warm, a fever broke out in the town, which was attributed to the heat of Smock Alley Theatre and the excitement of the performances on emotional people. It carried off vast numbers, and was long referred to as the Garrick fever.

In July Peg Woffington took her benefit, when she appeared as Lady Anne. Entertainments of dancing by Signora Barbarina were given between the acts of the tragedy, to which was added The Virgin Unmasked, "the part of Miss Lucy by Miss Woffington, with a new epilogue in the character of Miss Lucy wrote by Mr. Garrick." Woffington and Garrick continued to play until August, when they returned to London, highly satisfied, as Hitchcock states, "with the profit and reputation arising from this excursion, and delighted with the generous and hospitable reception they experienced from the nobility and gentry of this kingdom, and which they always acknowledged in the warmest terms." Whilst in Dublin Garrick "was caressed by all ranks of people as a theatrical phenomena." A dozen invitations of a night poured in on him from the hospitable gentry; his Sundays were bespoken weeks in advance; his praises, and those of Peg Woffington, were sung by ballad singers in every street; he was followed through the thoroughfares by admirers anxious to see him in his habit as he lived, and by beggars who desired to profit by his prosperity. This remarkable season ended on the 19th of August, a short time after which date he and

Peg Woffington, charmed by their reception and enriched by their visit, returned to London.

Meanwhile the Aungier Street Theatre had been well nigh deserted, for Mrs. Cibber no longer drew crowds, and after a final appearance as Andromache she left Ireland and the house was closed.

In the autumn both theatres opened their doors, each in its way bidding for success. Dissatisfaction having arisen regarding the affairs of Aungier Street, Mr. Swan was appointed as actor-manager, and began his *régime* by opening a subscription for the performance of eight of Shakespeare's plays. Duval, knowing from experience the perils of competition save when assisted by players of reputation, engaged a company of rope-dancers and tumblers, whom he rightly judged would attract the town and profit himself.

The manner in which he announced their performances reads quaintly enough. " This present evening, Tuesday, December 7th, 1842," says the playbill, " will be presented by the celebrated company of Germans, Dutch, Italians, and French, several feats of activity, consisting of rope-dancing, tumbling, vaulting, equilibres, and ground-dancing. Madame German performs on the rope with stilts (never done here), and will also perform on the slack rope. Monsieur Dominique will perform the surprising equilibres of the circle, never attempted by any but himself, in which he is drawn up forty feet high by his head, fires off two pistols, and is let down again in the same posture. Monsieur Dominique and Monsieur Guittar perform the surprising tumble over the double fountain. Monsieur Dominique tumbles through an hogshead of fire in the middle, and a lighted torch in each hand, &c."

That mountebanks should fill the stage where Garrick recently performed, was considered a desecration by many, especially by Swan, who hailed the opportunity of denouncing a rival and advertising himself in letters to the papers, in pamphlets, and in halting verse, to all of which came hot replies, the town taking one side or the other. The Shakesperian performances having come to an end, Swan engaged Dr. Arne and the company of singers under his direction, who were then giving concerts in Fishamble

Street, to perform in The Masque of Comus. Dr. Arne set the whole piece to new music and divided the choruses into parts, which had not previously been done. The manager took the principal part of Comus, and spoke the prologue, whilst the epilogue was delivered by Mrs. Furnival. The performance was produced on the 10th of January, 1743, and was received with the highest marks of applause. When its course was run several other musical pieces were placed upon this stage.

It was at this time—January 29th, 1743—that the character of Richard III. was played at Smock Alley Theatre by a young gentleman whose name was not announced, but who was destined after much strife and endeavour to bring about an important change in the condition of the Irish stage.

This young gentleman was Thomas Sheridan, son of Dr. Sheridan, a divine and a schoolmaster by profession, also a scholar, a poet, a musician, and an author; a good-natured man, ignorant of the value of money, which he could never keep, the dupe of many, indiscreet, unworldly, but something of a genius. His friend Dean

139

Swift declared him " the best instructor of youth in the three kingdoms and perhaps in Europe, and as great a master of the Greek and Latin languages. He had a very fruitful invention and a talent for poetry."

His eldest surviving son, Tom, who was destined to turn player, and to become the father of Richard Brinsley Sheridan, was educated at home until he reached his thirteenth year, when he was sent to Westminster School at a time when his parents could ill afford it. The boy's godfather, Dean Swift, narrates that Tom was immediately taken notice of upon examination, and although a mere stranger, was by pure merit elected a King's Scholar. Whilst his son was here Dr. Sheridan wrote to Swift that his school only supplied him with food without which he could not live. "I pray God," he says, "you may never feel a dun to the end of your life, for it is too shocking to the honest heart."

After this statement we are not surprised to learn that the Doctor was unable to add fourteen pounds " to enable his son to finish the year, which if he had done he would have been removed to a higher class, and in another year would have been sped off (as the phrase is) to a fellowship in Oxford or Cambridge. Being obliged to return to Ireland, the lad was sent to Trinity College, where through interest he was placed on the foundation, when he took his degree and studied for a fellowship.

Meanwhile the slovenly, indigent, cheerful Doctor fell ill of dropsy and asthma and died in 1738, the year in which his son took his degree. It was at first thought that the latter would fill his father's place as a schoolmaster, but the life was uncongenial and unsuited to young Sheridan, who resolved to try his fortune on the boards. His first appearance, Hitchcock states, "succeeded beyond the most sanguine expectations of the friends of our young candidate for fame, and equalled any first essay ever remembered by the oldest performers on the stage."

Thus encouraged, he next played Mithridates in the tragedy of that name, when, again succeeding, he threw aside his disguise and appeared for a second time as Richard, under his own name.

Personally he was well favoured, but his

movements were somewhat stiff, his face lacked expression, and his voice was hard and unsympathetic. His ambition was great and his manner engaging, save when under the influence of that temper which wrecked almost every undertaking of his life. During the remainder of the season he played such important parts as Brutus in Julius Cæsar, Carlos in The Fop's Fortune, and Cato in the tragedy of that name. Greatly admired, especially in serious parts, he drew large houses, and all went well with him and with the theatre for some time.

For the summer season Smock Alley Theatre passed into the temporary management of one Philips, whose repute for honesty was not of the best, and who engaged Theophilus Cibber, whose character has already been made known. The latter played in his father's comedies, and occasionally attempted tragic parts. Sheridan, who likewise continued to appear, disliked the management and bore no love to Cibber. One night in June when he was announced to appear as Cato, Sheridan on coming to the theatre found the whole establishment behind the curtain in a state of confusion. Scene shifters and carpenters were clamouring for unpaid wages; the band refused to play unless their arrears were discharged; the company grumbled, and at the same time news was brought that Philips had absconded.

Much depressed, Sheridan went to dress, but soon discovered that the robe in which he had played Cato only a couple of nights before was missing. He was then told that Philips had taken away the garment, and Sheridan came to the conclusion this was done to prevent him playing that night. "It has been said," he writes in a letter he addressed to the town, "that the want of a robe was a trifling thing, and that the audience would have been content to have received me in any dress; they must have but little skill in theatrical affairs, who think a proper habit is not absolutely necessary. This was more particularly my case in this character, as it is one for which I am naturally very unfit in my person, and in which nothing could have made my appearance supportable but a large robe to cover my defects, and give a gravity and dignity to my person, which I wanted, and which are so absolutely necessary to the character."

143

Sheridan, who was, as he declared, beside himself with passion, immediately hurried to Theophilus Cibber's dressing-room and asked him "what he should do in this exigence for want of a robe." Cibber answered shortly enough, "Play without one." Upon that, as Sheridan explained to the public in a letter already quoted from, "I laid open to him what a despicable figure I should make, when he turned upon his heel and said, ' Damn me if I care what you do, the play shall not stand still for you,' and immediately went and ordered the prompter to draw up the curtain. When I heard this I was stunned at the insolence of the fellow, who neither had any right to command in that house, nor was in any shape interested in the event of that night."

Sheridan rushed "like a madman precipitately on the stage " to explain to the audience that he could not play Cato that evening, when Cibber, following him, offered to read the part. Sheridan then declaring he would not again play at that house during the season, hurried home in a state of disorder. He then thought it necessary to publish an apology to the town for the disappointment he had occasioned, and at the same time to explain the circumstances which had forced him to act as he had done. And his case now being made public, his cause was warmly espoused by the College Boys, as the undergraduates were called.

The students of Trinity College were in those days a formidable body who delighted in riot, and whose normal condition was disorder. A protest made against their ways, the slightest interference offered to one of them, was enough to secure the vengeance of the whole, when, mighty in numbers and noisy with threats, they sallied forth, a compact, lawless throng, to chastise the offenders. The watch fled before them, and they who resisted were stabbed with swords or felled by the force of the keys of their rooms, which being tied to the sleeves or tails of their gowns, the students used with terrible effect.

On one occasion Thomas Mills, bookseller, and editor and printer of the *Hibernian Journal*, was rash enough to condemn their practices, when a few days later a coach drove up to his door containing four young gentlemen, who under pretence of bargaining for some books induced him to leave his shop, when he was immediately hustled into the coach and a pistol placed to his forehead with the threat of being shot if he called for help. Once inside the gates, he was hauled from the coach and surrounded by hundreds of yelling students, who almost trampled him to death in dragging him to a pump which stood in the centre of one of the quadrangles. Water was poured on his head until he was almost suffocated, and indeed he only escaped with his life through the interference of the Fellows. This offence was by no means visited with expulsion, but was merely noticed by an admonition which excused rather than condemned the barbarity.

Above all other men the hatred of the Gownsmen was most fiercely directed against bailiffs. The University was considered a sanctuary for debtors, and woe befell the bailiff found within its gates. When on a memorable occasion one of the offending tribe was caught prowling about the quadrangles, he was hurried with shouts of joy to the pump, where he was soused with hearty goodwill. Whilst his punishment was taking place, Dr. Wilder, a Fellow remarkable for his eccentricity, passed by, and seeing the sport, lustily cried out, " Gentlemen, gentlemen, for God's sake don't nail his ears to the pump." The hint was received with shouts of delight, nails and a hammer were sought for by a willing score of madcaps, and the bailiff, notwithstanding his prayers and shrieks, had his ears fixed to the pump by tenpenny nails.

When personal offenders were few, and a prospect of inglorious peace presented itself, the students, to keep their spirits up and their hands in practice, joined in the street fights which were continually being waged between the Liberty Boys, the weavers and tailors who lived in the upper part of the town, and the Ormond Boys, the butchers who lived on Ormond Quay and its districts.

These conflicts, which were a constant source of terror to all peace-loving people, usually began by the Liberty Boys rushing down Thomas Street Hill and making an onslaught on the butchers at the other side of the Liffey, who were always ready and willing to fight. The quays and bridges were the scene of these battles, which sometimes outlasting a day, were begun afresh on the morrow. All shops in the neighbourhood were closed, and stones and other missiles were flung far and wide, so that danger threatened spectators. Interference was neither expected nor received, for the watch were powerless against such numbers, and a Lord Mayor when once appealed to, declared it was " as much as his life was worth " to venture near the battle ; so that for days all intercourse between the north and south side of the city was suspended.

Life was frequently lost on such occasions ; but though the butchers used their knives freely, their desire was not to kill, but rather to " haugh," or cut a tendon of their enemies' legs, which left the victims lame for life. On the other hand, the Liberty Boys, when conquerors, delighted to drag their opponents to their own meat market, when, dislodging the carcases found hanging there, they hooked the butchers by the jaws and left them dangling above their stalls. On one occasion when a battle was fought and won, a number of College Boys were missing, and on being sought by their fellows were discovered hanging above the butchers stalls on iron hooks, from which, however, they were merely suspended by the waistbands of their breeches.

True to their traditions, the gownsmen now determined to champion Sheridan, who had once belonged to their body, and to summarily punish those who had ill-used him. Councils were called and preparations made, but before vengeance was wreaked they thought it advisable to address a letter to the editor of *Faulkner's Journal*, "to prevent any misconstructions we might possibly expose ourselves to." This letter informed the public that "upon a strict and impartial inquiry into the reasons of Mr Sheridan's not appearing on Thursday last in the character of Cato, we find them so strong and satisfactory that our resolution, we hope, will be favourably looked on of seeing him righted, and the insolence of others properly chastised, who either through envy or malice would remove the strongest inducement we have to visiting the playhouse, and consequently deprive us of the satisfaction we propose to ourselves from the most rational amusements;

and it is expected none will condemn us for frustrating the malicious contrivance of some designing wretches, and by so doing convince them their enviously shallow practices shall always prove abortive, whenever they tend to wrong or depress merit."

Another epistle addressed to Sheridan hoped that his just resentment would not deprive these polite young gentlemen who constituted themselves arbiters in the dispute, of the satisfaction they promised themselves from so eminent a genius; and as the declarations of some malicious persons might possibly have made him apprehensive of being hereafter insulted, they took an opportunity of publicly assuring him that they had determined not only to support him, but to frustrate the schemes that might be formed to his disadvantage.

Sheridan reading a declaration of war between the lines of these elegant epistles, and being anxious to prevent a riot in the theatre, hastened to Trinity College and besought the ringleaders to forego the pleasure of a free fight which they had promised themselves. This they eventually consented to, and would have sorrowfully kept peace even when such a desirable opportunity for warfare presented itself, had not a letter appeared from Mr. Theophilus Cibber, comedian, to Mr. Thomas Sheridan, tragedian, in which the writer, exhibited much of his native insolence. In this Sheridan was addressed as "Master Tommy" and "Dear Tommy"; his statements were declared false, his behaviour such as made it doubtful whether "the lowest body of people would choose him to mingle with him"; his acting so inferior that Cibber could scarcely believe the most indifferent troop of strolling players would care to rank with him. Then the two letters issued from Trinity College were said to be, if not *ipso facto* his, at least the work of a mistaken friend on whose good-nature he had imposed.

This insolent epistle drove the college boys to fury ; peace was scouted ; nothing could now prevent war. Excitement was heightened by news that Cibber had hired "a party of ruffians and other desperate fellows" to oppose them. Accordingly when on Thursday evening, the 21st of July, Cibber appeared as Othello, a

hoarse shout of hatred went up from the throats
of hundreds of youths. This was the signal for
opposition cheers from the party of hired
ruffians. Words were exchanged, quickly
followed by blows. Cibber stood silent watch-
ing the fray until a shower of oranges made him
beat a retreat. A cessation of hostilities followed,
to break out again with fuller fury on his re-
appearance ; a tumultuous riot ensued ; the pit
became a battlefield, the gods looking down
took part in the fight, not alone by yells of
encouragement or execration, but by missiles
which they rained upon the combaters. Candles
and lamps were smashed, clouds of dust filled
the air, blood flowed freely, until at last the
College Boys turned out the party of ruffians
and other desperate fellows, and followed their
retreat with threats of throwing them into the
malodorous Liffey.

In this way was Sheridan avenged. Moreover
reparation was made to his outraged dignity
when, by special command of their Excellencies
the Lords Chief Justices, he was announced to
appear as Cato at the Aungier Street Theatre
on the 28th July, it being his first appearance

on that stage and the last time of his performance for that season. On this night he
appeared with every sign of gratification and
delight before a crowded audience which numbered all the nobility and gentry then in town,
and received "every tribute of applause which
his late unfair treatment and masterly performance merited."

CHAPTER VII.

BOTH houses closed their doors in July, 1743,
whilst their companies betook themselves to the
provinces, to return in autumn. And now came
a new departure ; for the proprietors of both
theatres, seeing from experience that the town
was unable to support them separately, resolved
to unite their fortunes and their forces and play
in Aungier Street only. This resolution being
acted upon, a new company was formed from
the two already in existence. Those who were
not selected considered themselves wronged ;
their occupation was gone, and they had no
desire to seek another. Therefore joining
together, they obtained the old lease of Smock

Alley by fraudulent means, Hitchcock thinks, took possession of that house, and determined to offer every opposition to their late comrades.

In forming their company, the joint proprietors wished to engage Sheridan, and had offered him a hundred pounds for the season, guaranteeing him an equal sum as the result of his benefit. These terms by no means pleased him, for they were fifty pounds less than they proposed to give Mrs. Furnival, the leading lady, and about a third of what they gave Dr. Arne, who conducted musical pieces, and Mr. Lowe, who sang in them. In declining the proffered salary, Sheridan on his part made a suggestion, namely that he would undertake the entire management, as the result of which he promised to secure them five hundred pounds for the season.

This they promptly rejected, when he went over to the Smock Alley company, that had meanwhile reinforced its numbers by engaging a company then acting in the north. The Aungier Street United Company of Comedians opened their doors on the 11th of October, when by command of their Graces the Duke and Duchess of Devonshire, The Conscious Lovers was performed. It was not until the third of the following month that the Smock Alley Theatre announced its first night under the new management, when Sheridan played Richard the Third; Elrington, King Henry; and "all the rest of the parts by persons who never appeared on this stage."

Fierce opposition was now carried on, though it lasted a short time, for so destitute of merit was the company Sheridan had elected to join, that competition became impossible. He therefore left Smock Alley and soon after was engaged to play at Covent Garden, and made his first appearance on the English stage on the 31st March, 1744. Nearly twelve months previously Garrick had proposed to him that he should come to London, and that they should play in the same house.

In reply, Sheridan wrote him a long and friendly letter, dated 21st April, 1743, in which he heartily thanks David for his invitation to pass the summer with him at Walton, "though I could wish," he adds, "you had not mentioned it, for it has given me no small concern that the posture of my affairs will not permit me to enjoy that happiness." He has not fixed on any scheme for the coming winter, but he has been offered such advantageous terms as will, he believes, keep him in Dublin till January. Then comes the pith of his letter.

" As to your proposal of our playing together," he writes, " I am afraid I have too many powerful reasons against it ; a well cut pebble may pass for a diamond till a fine brilliant is placed near it, and puts it out of countenance. Besides, we should clash so much in regard to characters, that I am afraid it is impossible we can be in the same house. Richard, Hamlet, and Lear, as they are your favourite characters, are mine also ; and though you were so condescending as to say I might appear in any part of yours, yet I question whether the town would bear to see a worse performer in one of your characters in the same house with you, though they might endure him in another.

" I have a scheme to propose to you, which at first view may seem a little extraordinary to you, but if rightly considered, must turn to both our advantages. If you could be brought to divide your immortality with me, we might, like Castor and Pollux, appear always in different hemispheres (now I think on't, I don't know whether the old simile of the two buckets would not do as well, but that is beneath the dignity of a tragedian): in plain English, what think you of dividing the kingdoms between us — to play one winter in London and another in Dublin?

" I have many reasons to offer in favour of this scheme, which will not come within the compass of a letter; I shall only say that it will make us always new in both kingdoms, and consequently always more followed; and I am satisfied that Dublin is as well able to pay one actor for the winter as London."

On Sheridan's withdrawal from Smock Alley, its company collapsed, and the theatre passed into the control of the Aungier Street management, so that opposition was no longer possible.

At this time another Irish actor arose to give distinction to the British stage. This was Spranger Barry, the descendant of a good old Irish family that had lately taken to trade. Spranger Barry's father was an honest silversmith, and had bred his son to follow the

same calling. In due time the elder was succeeded by the younger, and it was not until he
was six-and-twenty that he became a player,
for which he was particularly fitted by nature.

Close upon six feet high, he was elegantly
shaped, and his natural bearing was full of
grace and dignity. His features were regular,
his eyes bright and blue, his hair was pale gold,
whilst the extraordinary mobility of his face
gave expression to every sentence he spoke.
For " mere human beauty " he was said never
to have been surpassed. But perhaps his chief
charm was his voice, the sweetest that ever
sounded on man's lips, which gained him the
appellation of "the silver-tongued." Arthur
Murphy, the dramatist, declared that Barry
" could wheedle a bird off the bush " ; Hitchcock
says " the harmony and melody of his silver
tones were resistless "; whilst an anonymous
critic avowed that "all exquisitely tender or
touching writing came mended from his mouth.
There was a pathos, a sweetness, a delicacy in
his utterance which stole upon the mind and
forced conviction on the memory. Every
sentiment of honour and virtue, recommended
to the ear by the language of the author,

was riveted to the heart by the utterance of Barry."

His first appearance was made on the 15th of February, 1744, when it was announced that the tragedy of Othello would be acted by his Majesty's Company of Comedians at the Theatre Royal in Smock Alley, the part of Othello to be performed by Mr. Barry, whilst Mrs. Bayly would act Desdemona, and Mr. Lowe and Mme. Chateauneuf furnish entertainments of dancing and singing between the acts. For weeks previously rumour had spread through the town that the silversmith of Skinner Row was going to play tragedy, and the consequent excitement was great. When the curtain rose a full house was ready to greet and encourage him. A people so susceptible to beauty of form and music of voice would have given a hearty reception to such a man no matter how grievously wanting he might be in the art he essayed, but when to such physical gifts as his were added amazing talents, the enthusiasm he gained may readily be imagined. Loud and long was the applause which awarded each fresh attempt of his to realize the love and jealousy of the Moor.

One who at a later date saw him in this character, says he was "master of the quick vicissitudes of love, of grief, of rage and tenderness; and in the conflict, or, as Shakespeare has it, in the tempest and whirlwind of the passions, his voice was harmony in an uproar." The sympathetic audience of this first night were in raptures, and their delight was as great as their surprise. Men held their breath at the outpourings of his fury, and women were melted by the tenderness of his love. Nothing would satisfy the audience, thrilled by the emotions he awoke, but his promise to gratify his admirers by a repetition of his performance.

To this crowds flocked in numbers that would have twice filled the theatre. Endeavours to gain admittance were conducted with a good-humour that occasionally gave way to strife, and the cheers which greeted his first entrance as the Moor were as loud and lusty as had ever before welcomed actor on that stage.

Later in the season further entertainment was given at this house by the engagement of

Samuel Foote. Though at this time little known as an actor, he had gained considerable reputation as a young man of fashion gifted with sprightly humour and abundant wit. Whilst yet an undergraduate at Oxford, he had proved himself to possess originality. Leaving the university without troubling to take his degrees, he entered the Temple, where he disdained to study law, preferring to burst upon the town as a full-blown dandy. The length of his bagwig, the shape of his sword, the fineness of his lace, and the colour of his muff, were matters that occupied his consideration.

Habited in a green suit bedizened with silver, a great bouquet in his breast, he frequented the fashionable coffee-houses and wine taverns, the observed of all, the admired of many. Here he bandied words with the wittiest, set his companions in a roar with his mimicry, made popular idols and solemn humbugs wince under the dainty lash of his satire. Having inherited a fortune, he spent it freely. At the playhouses wine taverns and gambling clubs he was a well-known figure. And as he was open-handed to all, he was followed by numbers; none more hospitable lived; pleasure became his pursuit, and extravagance landed him in the Fleet.

His stay here was brief, but on regaining liberty he realized that he had lost his followers. And as he was without money he set about making some. The example of David Garrick, son of an officer, appealed to Samuel Foote, who was descended from an ancient family, and though the latter at this period did not recognize the value of his mimicry as an element of attraction, he resolved to seek his fortune on the stage.

News of this determination flying through the town, his appearance was awaited with impatience. To this was added amusement when it became known that Foote, small and insignificant of stature, with the merry eyes of a wit, and the facile expression of a humorist, was announced to play Othello, the Moor of Venice, "dressed after the manner of the country." Nothing more laughable than his performance could be imagined, the unconsciousness of his burlesque being the germ of the entertainment. This his first appearance

was made on the 6th of February, 1744, at the
Haymarket, and so little was he aware of his
unsuitability for the part, that he repeated it
three or four times. His next attempt was as
Lord Foppington in the Relapse, and here his
mimicry proved serviceable, inasmuch as his
playing resembled Colley Cibber's in the same
comedy.

As an actor he gave no promise of the
success he was later to secure; and it was
without much reputation as a player that he
made his bow to a Dublin audience.

Hitchcock tells us that Foote " brought a few
crowded audiences and was well received " ; but
his engagement was short, and he created little
sensation in the capital where his antics were
later to cause universal diversion.

Though Aungier Street and Smock Alley
Theatres were now under one management,
plays being given at either house alternately,
they were not long left to enjoy the monopoly
of entertaining the town. For the players who
had been driven from the latter house on
Sheridan's departure from amongst them, becoming desperate in their fight for an existence they considered necessary, took posses-

sion of a little theatre which had been erected for them in Capel Street. In this project they were joined by a few of the Aungier Street actors who were discontented with their situation. The Capel Street playhouse was opened on the 17th of January, 1745, when The Merchant of Venice was performed.

Hitchcock writes that though there were a few persons of merit in this new-formed community, yet " ill accommodated and destitute of wardrobe and scenery, there was not the least probability of standing against any such established company ; accordingly they languished for a few years and then gradually sank into obscurity."

Meanwhile, the old-established theatres failed to gain prosperity. As has been stated, Foote's visit was brief, and though Spranger Barry drew good houses whenever he played, his appearances were not frequent, for being a young actor, he had to study and rehearse new parts, whilst it was feared his Othello would pall by constant repetition. The principal cause of the decline of the theatre lay with those most concerned in its affairs. Its gentlemen proprietors, sometimes termed managers, numbered three and thirty, under whom acted seven other directors, ironically called by the public the seven wise men.

The diversity of opinion and interests of these individuals, together with their inexperience and consequent inability to judge what would succeed, brought the Irish stage into a lamentable state of decay, from which it was only temporarily rescued by the appearance of such players as Peg Woffington, Garrick, Tom Sheridan, and Barry. It now, however, seemed to have reached its lowest depths. At times not twenty persons were seen in the pit, the boxes were empty, for naturally enough the nobility and gentry did not care to see the same old pieces performed by indifferent players, and throughout the season of 1745 there were not three nights when the money taken covered the costs of the performance. Nay, for three successive weeks the audience was so sparse, that it was either dismissed or no plays were given out for future nights. Moreover, the poor actors secured but half their wretched salaries, the remaining half being retained as security for the expenses of their benefits.

The idea of closing the theatres altogether was seriously considered ; but as an alternative to this, and by public request, the managers asked Sheridan to return and take upon himself the sole direction of the stage ; they voluntarily offering to vest him with unlimited authority to act in every respect as he should think proper. " This," says Hitchcock, " was the only atonement in their power for a long series of ill-conduct and imprudence ; but this, indeed, compensated for all their former efforts.'

Sheridan was not unwilling to listen to the overtures made him, for whilst acting at Drury Lane, jealousy had arisen between him and Garrick, whom he regarded as his rival ; and though no hostilities were exhibited on either side, yet their friendship had gradually cooled. A change was therefore desirable for Sheridan ; and that such a change would place him in a position of supreme command, was gratifying to a man of his temperament.

Accordingly he said farewell to London and returned to Dublin full of laudable schemes for the advancement of the stage, the execution of which was to bring him much trouble and small profit.

No man was more suited for the task he undertook ; a task which, as will be shown, was fraught with difficulty and danger. In an uncommon measure he possessed tact, an invaluable quality in his new position. It became his endeavour to convince others of the necessity and usefulness of what he desired, and to request rather than command ; but forced to exert them, he was capable of showing firmness and determination. His courage was only equalled by his perseverance ; his excellent education gave broadness to his mind ; his social position entitled him to that respect generally withheld from those of his calling. Well read in the literature of the drama, he was enabled to select what was fittest for the stage, to which, above all, he was passionately devoted.

The difficulties he had to encounter in his new position are set down not only by himself but by Benjamin Victor, his assistant manager, and by Hitchcock, the historian of the Irish stage. At this time the players showed the uttermost indifference towards summonses for rehearsals. For those who had principal parts to present themselves at all was considered a polite attention; to appear when a play was half gone through, was in itself a merit. None of them, high or low, regarded punctuality as necessary. The slovenly and indifferent manner in which they acted was the cause of many strange blunders and mishaps at the evening performances. The chief cause of their negligence was due to the uncertainty felt of receiving their salaries; for where was the use of bothering if they were to get "nothing at all" for their work?

Such rehearsals as took place were usually attended by the young bloods about town; idle and dissolute fellows, who resorted here for mischief and diversion; as also by the college boys, who prided themselves as patrons of the drama, and judges of how a speech should be delivered. Victor tells us he had seen "actors and actresses rehearsing within a circle of forty or fifty of those young gentlemen whose time ought to have been better employed." Then the furniture and fittings of the stage were seldom taken into consideration; one poor canvas scene doing duty for fifty different acts in plays of widely differing dates; whilst the characters personated were dressed according to the taste and inclination of the players. Indeed, it was not an uncommon occurrence to see some of the personages in a Shakesperian tragedy in mediæval costume, whilst others wore the dress of the day.

As for the theatre itself, Sheridan states it "was looked upon as a common, and the actors as *feræ Naturâ*. One part of the house was a bear garden and the other a brothel. To such an absurd height had popular prejudice risen, that the owners were considered as having no property there but what might be destroyed at the will and pleasure of the people; that the actors had not the common privileges of British subjects, but were actual slaves; and that neither the one nor the other were under the protection of the laws."

Frequently it happened that whilst the pit was half empty and but a single row of the middle gallery was filled, over a hundred men of quality, students, bloods, and coffee-house critics, invaded the stage; mixing with the players so as scarcely to be distinguished from them, lounging at the wings so as to hinder the entrances and exits of the actors, or congregating in the background, where they passed free-and-easy comments on the performance, or otherwise hindered it by exchanging greetings and remarks with each other across the stage or with their friends in the boxes.

When, during his visit to Dublin, Garrick was playing Lear to the Cordelia of Peg Woffington, and they had come to that part of the tragedy where the distraught king is found asleep, his head supported by Cordelia's lap, they were suddenly disturbed, just as the curtain was about to be drawn, by a gay and gallant youth, who flung himself down beside Peg Woffington and treated her to specimens of his pretty wit. Peg turned on him wrathfully, and he, forgetting his gallantry, abused her roundly, whilst Garrick with great discretion kept silent. He looked at the fellow, however, with such indignation, that his glance was considered an affront by the fine gentleman, who hastened away in search of two comrades, with whom, when the play was over, he searched the house for Garrick, vowing with dreadful imprecations that they would put him to death.

On another night a merry young gentleman took it into his head to entertain himself by cutting to pieces with his sword a scene which had been newly painted. The theatre at the time had been let by Duval to a company of actors, and one of these, seeing the outrage, in a very humble manner begged that the young gentleman would desist, telling him the scene had cost a poor set of men a great deal of money, and that they could not give their performance, upon which they greatly depended, without its use. The young blood being wildly incensed by such interference, with furious oaths demanded how dared a player talk to a gentleman, flourished his sword, and would have wounded if not killed the actor had not those around interfered.

The fact was that every idler with a laced coat and a sword, that every stripling who had acquaintance with the actors and could afford a shilling bribe, or any bully who could rap out an oath and flourish an oak sapling, was sure to

gain admission behind the scenes. The upper
gallery was a source of vexation and terror to
the poor players. To this part of the house the
liveried chair-bearers and footmen were free to
resort whilst they waited for their employers ;
and here also the public gained entrance by the
payment of twopence. As accommodation was
limited, the crush on certain nights was great ;
those who paid resented the presence of those
who had free admission, whereon fights followed
that deafened the house and frequently interrupted the performance.

Soon after his arrival in Dublin, Sheridan
called a full board of proprietors and acquainted
them with his views. He clearly stated that
the best actors in the world, whilst the
stage was crowded with rude and boisterous
spectators, and whilst there were perpetual
tumults and uproars in the gallery, could
neither exert their own talents properly, nor
afford any rational entertainment to the sober
and sensible part of mankind. He saw that it
was curiosity alone that drew crowds to see
actors of eminence, "in the same manner as
people go to see shows and monsters once, but

return to them no more." And it was evident to him that whilst the stage was in such a wretched state of slavery, it must in general be ill-supplied, and the entertainments of course be proportionately defective. But at the same time he believed that if order succeeded to anarchy and decorum to brutality, that if the theatre was under sanction of the law and the performers allowed to enjoy the common privileges of British subjects, the dramatic entertainments might make speedy progress to perfection, and the number of the audiences increased by the frequent presence of the grave, the regular, the sober part of mankind. Moreover, then "the profession of an actor would not only lose the unmerited disgrace which had been affixed to it, but in time might become reputable, by being supplied with persons of genteel education, improved talents, and good behaviour."

His task of reforming the stage was considered chimerical, though all were willing he should try the experiment. He therefore undertook the sole management of the two theatres, and later by letters of attorney he gave Benjamin Victor equal powers with himself to direct business and become treasurer. His first act was to introduce a new table of laws and " to convince the actors that nothing but a due observance of them could by degrees raise them from that contempt which they had hitherto so justly deserved and met with."

To the credit of the actors, be it stated that, seeing how judicious and earnest were his ideas, how tactful and beneficial his acts, they generally supported him in his endeavours. Personally he set the example of punctuality at rehearsals, which he fixed at such reasonable hours as might suit the attendance of all, so that he was seldom obliged to enforce obedience by forfeits—a system so disagreeable to him, that he preferred to part with the services of those who persisted in being late rather than deprive them of their earnings. At these rehearsals he attended to the business of each scene, made suggestions regarding the manner in which speeches and phrases were delivered, and insisted that everything should be gone through as it would during the evening performance.

And so far as was possible he dressed the

characters of the plays he produced in appropriate costumes, and furnished and decorated the stage in a manner that was then considered elegant. " Indeed," says Hitchcock, " he has frequently been blamed for launching into expenses which the profits of the performance were unable to repay."

The departure from old traditions which gave most satisfaction to his company, was that the salaries of all connected with the theatre were regularly paid on Saturdays, a fund for the purpose being established to secure the continuance of this rule, no matter what the fortunes of the management. In all ways, indeed, he studied the interests of those he employed, and his highest ambition centred itself in being considered the father of his company.

Before beginning his season he thought it advisable to strengthen his forces by engaging David Garrick, already a favourite with the town, and George Anne Bellamy, a young actress who had recently made a sensation in London. Sheridan's desire to engage Garrick showed a broadness of mind and freedom from jealousy unusual in one of his· calling, for both

excelled in the performance of the same
characters, and whilst the former was in
London they had been regarded as rivals. In
writing to Garrick the new manager said that
"understanding he had expressed a wish to pay
a second visit to Ireland, he should be happy to
see him in Dublin, and that he would give him
every advantage and encouragement he could
in reason expect." The terms proposed were
that they should divide the profits arising from
their joint performance after deducting the
expenses incurred. And bearing in mind the
coolness that had existed between them in
London, Sheridan added that Garrick "must
expect nothing from his friendship, but all that
the best actor had a right to command he
might be very certain should be granted."

It happened that when Garrick received this
letter he was in the company of his friend
Colonel Wyndham, into whose hand he placed
it, saying it was the oddest epistle he had ever
read in his life. The Colonel, on perusing it
answered that it might be an odd, but it was
surely an honest communication, adding, "
should certainly depend upon a man that

treated me with that openness and simplicity of heart." Eventually Garrick decided on playing in Dublin, though he did not make his appearance until the December of that year—1745—two months after Sheridan had begun his season.

Before that time George Anne Bellamy had made her bow to a Dublin audience.

CHAPTER VIII.

George Anne Bellamy—Strange career—She becomes a
 player—Appearance in Dublin—Sheridan's brilliant
 season—Miss Bellamy quarrels with Garrick—Lord
 Chesterfield and the playhouse—St. Leger's im-
 pertinence—Garrick's farewell—Miss Bellamy under-
 goes a social trial.

THE annals of the drama or the chronicles of
romance contain no pages more diverting than
the memoirs of George Anne Bellamy. Her
father, Lord Tyrawley, an Irish peer of brilliant
talents, handsome presence, and reckless extravagance, eloped with her mother, Miss Sale, when
she was a pupil at a fashionable boarding-school
in Queen's Square, London.

George Anne, who was born at Fingal, was
taken from her mother at an early age, and
when about four was sent to school in Boulogne
where she remained some seven years. At the
end of that time she was summoned to London

by her father, who had been acting as British Ambassador to Portugal, when he showed her great affection, and introduced her to his distinguished friends. In a little while he was appointed Ambassador to Russia, when he placed his daughter in charge of a woman of quality, whom he remunerated with a hundred a year. The girl was forbidden to hold communication with her mother, a worthless slattern, who had gone on the stage and married twice since her parting with Tyrawley. The woman, however, sought a private interview with her child, whom she induced to live with her believing the ambassador would allow her the sum he was paying for his daughter's support.

The latter on coming to live with her mother brought all the money and jewels she possessed ; but the first was quickly spent and the latter pawned ; and when application was made for funds to Tyrawley, he declined to send them or to hold communication with the disobedient girl. Mother and daughter were in sore distress when the former met Peg Woffington out walking one day, and having known the great actress in Dublin, she appealed to her for help. This was freely given by Peg Woffington, who also invited mother and daugher to visit her at Teddington. Whilst there, a play was got up and acted in a barn for the benefit of the neighbours around, parts being taken by Garrick, Peg Woffington, her sister Polly, and George Anne Bellamy, when the latter showed signs of talent.

On her return to town she made the acquaintance of the daughters of John Rich, manager of Covent Garden, and was one day reciting to them some speeches of Othello, when Rich passing that way, paused to hear, applauded, and declared if she studied for the stage he would give her an engagement.

Being as good as his word, she was soon cast for the part of Monimia in The Orphan for a performance at Covent Garden. In years and appearance she was a child, and James Quin declined to play the hero of a tragedy to such a heroine. The remainder of the company followed his example, and refused to attend rehearsals. They were eventually brought to their senses by the infliction of heavy fines, and Quin was induced to represent Chamont. The performance was announced for the 22nd November, 1744, and though her name was not given in the bill, it was generally known who was the young player.

As the daughter of a peer representing his Majesty in Russia, as one who had roused a storm in the green-room and won favourable predictions from the manager, she excited much interest and curiosity, and a brilliant house assembled to witness her first appearance. This came close to being a failure, for seized by stage fright, she stood before the house silent as a statue and as incapable of movement, until the curtain was dropped on the scene. When raised once more, the same embarrassment held her, but being encouraged by the house, she gradually recovered, acted with spirit, and gained the applause of all, including Quin, who lifting her in his arms, declared she had "the true spirit within her."

She repeated her performance next evening, and played at Covent Garden during the season at the end of which time a wicked old man, Lord Byron, grand-uncle to the poet, ran away

with her by strategy in the most dramatic
manner possible. Her mother, who had become
deeply religious, failed to believe George Anne's
protestations of innocence, the consequence being
the latter fell ill of grief and vexation. Scarce
had she recovered when Sheridan, who had been
acquainted with her whilst in London, offered to
engage her; and being anxious to leave town
where scandal had attacked her, and desirous
to seek the support of her country-people,
she at once accepted his terms and joined
his ranks.

No sooner had she arrived in Dublin than she
hastened to wait on Lord Tyrawley's sister, Mrs.
O'Hara. The latter was mightily displeased
that George Anne had become a player, but at
the same time proposed to introduce her to the
fashionable world as her niece. Mrs. O'Hara
was an invalid, who was moreover afflicted
with blindness, and therefore could be of little
service socially to the actress, but the kind old
lady soon made George Anne acquainted with
the Hon. Mrs. Butler, sister-in-law to my Lord
Lanesborough, a bright, bustling, gaily-dressed
woman, with an elegant figure, who was a person

of the first rank and importance. Good-natured to a rare degree, she was willing to extend her patronage to Miss Bellamy, who was accordingly bidden to Mrs. Butler's house, which was frequented by most of the nobility.

Sheridan had now a strong company with which to begin his campaign ; for not only was he a great favourite, but Garrick, Barry, and Bellamy were sure to draw crowded houses, whilst he had also engaged such useful and capable players as Mrs. Furnival, Mrs. Walker Frank Elrington, Vanderbank, Sparks, Morris, and others well known to the town.

Sheridan's first season as a manager began in October, 1745, and after a few weeks he introduced Miss Bellamy to the town, she making her *début* on the Aungier Street stage on the 11th of November. The play selected for the occasion was The Orphan, she representing Monimia to the Chamont of Sheridan and the Castalio of Barry. Young and beautiful, with a flexible voice and a graceful demeanour, Miss Bellamy favourably impressed her audience, and was rewarded by uncommon applause. Her second appearance was as Desdemona to Sheridan's

184

Othello, when her pathos drew tears from the women of quality who had crowded to see her.

On the 24th of November Garrick landed in Dublin. Though he had enlisted under Sheridan's management, he was not quite satisfied with the terms proffered, that of sharing profits or losses on the nights he played, and preferred a stipulated sum for performing during the winter. This Sheridan was unwilling to give, stating that the original offer was fairer, for then he would receive half of what he brought to the house.

A dispute then arose between them, which the manager was unwilling should continue; so taking out his watch, he told Garrick he must have his decision in five minutes, on which David agreed to share the profits.

On the 9th of December he appeared as Hamlet, Mrs. Storer playing Ophelia, and Mrs. Furnival the Queen, when his reception "was such as his extraordinary merit deserved." He next appeared as Richard the Third, a character that he and Sheridan played alternately; and each subsequently represented Iago to the Othello of Barry.

Presently it was proposed that King John should be revived, the manager and Garrick to play the King and the Bastard on alternate nights. Now Miss Bellamy greatly desired to appear as Constance, and indeed had stipulated in her agreement that she should play this part. To this, however, Garrick strongly objected, on the plea that she was too young ; he desiring it should be given to an older and more experienced actress, Mrs. Furnival.

On this Miss Bellamy poutingly flew to her patroness, who, though she greatly esteemed Garrick, resolved to champion her protegé and punish David. As a woman of consequence she possessed great power in the genteel world, which she now exerted ; for she immediately sent round word to all her friends requesting they would not attend the playhouse when King John was performed. One and all obeyed, for not only were they willing to oblige her, but as she frequently gave balls and routs that were the talk of the town, they knew that to prove heedless of her commands was to exile themselves from her assemblies.

Accordingly when the play was performed,

186

Garrick, who was accustomed to see thronged houses, was dismayed to find empty circles and deserted boxes. And not alone did his pride, but, what was as important to him, his pocket suffer, for the receipts of the house did not amount to forty pounds. The result was that Miss Bellamy was besought to play Constance, when Mrs. Butler was gracious enough to permit and sanction the presence of her friends at the performance, when more people were turned away than could gain places, and the dispute relative to the characters having become known to the town, she was received with the warmest marks of appreciation.

Now Garrick was a man who loved peace, especially when it profited him, and on the date coming round on which he was to take the first of his two benefits, the 20th December, he selected Jane Shore for the occasion, and begged that George Anne would play that character. But this spoilt young actress had not yet recovered from her indignation at David's recent behaviour, and was determined to return the mortification he had caused her. Therefore, tossing high her pretty head, she replied that as she was too young to act Constance, she was likewise too juvenile to represent Jane Shore.

Garrick was not, however, willing to accept this answer, for knowing the advantage of securing the fashionable people who supported her, he desired her to appear in the play. He therefore waited on Mrs. Butler and begged that she would induce Miss Bellamy to accede to his wishes. And that he might further conciliate her, he penned her a letter, in which amongst other things he said that if she would oblige him, he would write her a goody-goody epilogue, which with the help of her eyes would do more mischief than ever the flesh or the devil had done since the world began. This epistle he directed " To my Soul's Idol, the Beautified Ophelia," and handed it to his servant with orders to deliver it to Miss Bellamy.

It happened that the fellow had matter to attend more agreeable than Garrick's commands, so instead of obeying his master he gave the letter to a porter without looking at the address, telling him to hand it to the person whose name it bore. The porter, suspecting some joke, carried it to George Faulkner, the proprietor of a daily paper, who being glad to receive such copy, clapped it into his columns, to the confusion of David and the mirth of the town. Eventually Garrick was not only successful in securing Miss Bellamy for the evening of his benefit, but he likewise obtained the patronage of Lord Chesterfield for that occasion. Never was Viceroy more popular than his lordship, whose policy was to study and understand the Irish people. Finding them peaceably disposed and loyal, he treated them with a mildness and toleration that won their affection and confidence. He it was who during his vice-royalty indignantly rejected the harsh measures it was proposed he should use towards Catholics on the outbreak of the Scotch rebellion in the spring of 1745 ; and a story is told that at this time when a frightened official rushed into the Earl's room one morning with news that the people of Connaught were certainly rising, Lord Chesterfield coolly took out his watch, saying, "It's now nine o'clock and time for them to rise, so I'm inclined to believe your intelligence is true."

When visiting the playhouse he drove in

state with his coach and six, his outriders and footmen, his suite following in a line of emblazoned carriages, the whole procession attended by a company of troopers that scampered noisily through the badly paved streets, where crowds cheered lustily, and an army of ragged youths and brazen beggars scampered in the wake of so much splendour and glory.

Arriving at the theatre this evening, he was met at the door by Sheridan and Garrick, who waited on him candles in hand ready to conduct him to his box with its curtains of crimson tied back with gold tassels, the Royal arms showing on its front. In acknowledgment of their deferential bows, his lordship was graciously pleased to speak very kindly to Sheridan, but he took no notice whatever of Garrick, strange conduct in so polite a man, which Tom Davis, who mentions the occurrence, sets down to his lordship's policy of endearing himself to the Irish by smiling on an actor of their race, whilst ignoring a greater player who was English.

The moment the Viceroy was seen the house rose to greet him, the gallery cheered, the pit was in commotion, whilst smiling and bowing he graciously acknowledged the plaudits of the warm-hearted audience. Then the band struck up "God Save the King," after which the performance began.

It was on this night that an incident occurred that created some commotion. As yet Sheridan had been unable to rid the stage of the gallants who crowded it during the performance. Now one of these, young St. Leger, being heated with wine and stirred by Miss Bellamy's beauty, kissed the back of her neck as she passed him in full sight of the audience; whereon in a second she turned and smacked him full in the face. At this the Lord Lieutenant rose in his box and heartily clapped his hands, an example the audience was not slow to follow, the performance being stopped the while. Nor was this all, for at the conclusion of the act Lord Chesterfield sent Major Macartney, one of his suite, to St. Leger, requesting that he would make a public apology for his want of manners, which was accordingly done.

Garrick played Othello for his second benefit, and left Ireland on the 3rd of May, 1746, never more to return; and about a fortnight later

Sheridan closed his first season, which Hitchcock declares "the most honourable and brilliant that had then ever marked the Irish dramatic annals."

The fact that such players as Garrick, Sheridan, Barry, and Bellamy were seen on the same stage was a great step towards establishing a reputation that had fallen low. All ranks of people crowded the theatre, where, however, performances were seldom given more than twice a week. In the beginning of the season an application had been made to the manager, in reply to which he inserted the following in the daily papers : " Several ladies and gentlemen of distinction having applied to the proprietors of the theatre that ladies might be admitted into the *pit* at the same price as gentlemen are, which is the custom in London, and in every town in Ireland but Dublin, the said proprietors being willing to *oblige* all persons who encourage theatrical performances, have given orders that for the future ladies *will be admitted into the pit accordingly*."

The plays produced were freed from the indecencies which had previously disfigured them, and amusement was placed on a rational footing, the result being, as Sheridan afterwards stated, that "there have been sometimes more than thirty clergymen in the pit at a time, many of them deans and doctors of divinity, though formerly none of that order had ever entered the doors, unless a few who skulked in the gallery disguised. Persons venerable for age, station and character appeared frequently in the boxes and gave a sanction to the reformation."

The financial results were not so satisfactory, for the whole receipts of the season did not exceed three thousand four hundred pounds. Yet not disheartened, the hopeful manager entered into engagements to the extent of five thousand pounds and upwards for the following season.

Meanwhile Miss Bellamy had been enjoying herself mightily; women of fashion and consequence entertained her at dinners and parties, whilst innumerable gallants paid their homage to this fair young player who attracted universal attention. Whilst in the height of her social popularity, she was destined to undergo a trial which presents a picture of the manner of the times, that is worthy of attention.

One night whilst playing Lady Townley in The Provoked Husband, she received a note from Mrs. Butler, requesting that when at liberty she would come to her patroness without fail. As the letter was delivered during the performance, George Anne sent back a verbal message saying the fatigue of the evening would prevent her from being able to do herself the honour suggested. In a little while came a second note stating that Miss Bellamy must absolutely hasten to Stephen's Green the moment she had finished, and without waiting to change her dress.

This peremptory command excited her curiosity and compelled her obedience; so that no sooner had she quitted the stage than she got into her chair and was carried to Mrs. Butler's mansion. And just as she entered the drawing-room by one door, in trooped Colonel Butler and his male guests by another, they having just risen from the supper table. Mrs. Butler's manner was chilly, whilst the brilliant company of her sex who surrounded her did not deign to notice the actress. Wounded by a reception so unusual, she inquired its cause, when her hostess replied that a few minutes would determine whether she would ever notice her again.

This bewildered her the more, but her pride being piqued, she assumed an appearance of tranquillity. Now amongst the men who had entered was one whose shape and dress exceeded anything she had ever seen before, so elegant were they. Soon the attention of " this beautiful stranger " fixed itself upon her, and presently he introduced himself with an air so easy and confident that she immediately surmised he had travelled. In this she was not mistaken, for soon he acquainted her that he had just returned from making the grand tour, and was now about to take possession of his estate and settle for the remainder of his days in Dublin. They then entered into pleasant conversation, which was ultimately interrupted, when the gallant, full of curiosity, sought his hostess and in a whisper inquired who was the charming young lady that had held him in discourse.

" Surely you must know," said Mrs. Butler loudly, " I am certain you know her, nay, that you are well acquainted with her."

Though somewhat disconcerted by this reply, made in so audible a tone, he answered that he had never seen the young lady before and was anxious to discover her name.

At this the hostess became more agitated, and in a yet louder voice said, " Fie, fie, Mr. Medlicote. What can you say for yourself when I tell you that this is the dear girl whose character you so cruelly aspersed at supper? "

The confusion of this gallant, who had boasted of having received favours which he no doubt considered his attractions could win, was impossible to describe, whilst the young actress was equally overcome by confusion. Before either could recover, Mrs. Butler swept majestically across the room and embraced her in the most cordial manner, telling her the trial she had gone through was necessary, for had the man who traduced her seen her first in the theatre, there was no doubt he would have backed his assertions with oaths. George Anne had therefore been sent for at once that her innocence might be proved with a fulness of triumph, a promptness, and dramatic effect worthy of the stage, and appropriate to the fall of the curtain.

196

CHAPTER IX.

Sheridan's second season—Departure of Barry—The adventures of Miss Bellamy's silver tissue suit—Nancy O'Brian's hot blood—A young buck in the green room—Sheridan is abused—Riots in the theatre—Vengeance of the college boys—Trial of the offenders—Sheridan on his dignity.

IN opening his second season, Sheridan continued to have the support of Miss Bellamy, though he had lost that of Spranger Barry, who for some time had been dissatisfied with his position in Aungier Street Theatre.

In a letter written by him on the 6th of June, 1746, to David Garrick, he speaks of being overwhelmed with anxiety of mind, " being totally unable to remit the money you so kindly advanced." He then gives news of the theatre, and tells how Sheridan, to whom he bears no good will, had resolved to act Henry IV. for his benefit. On this occasion " Mr. Watson, who was to have played the part of

Poins, was fortunately taken ill; ten pounds in the house at seven o'clock; and finding Sheridan desirous of laying hold of Watson's illness as an excuse to put off the play, I proposed in the presence of many of his collegiate admirers then in the green room, to read the part of Poins, as it did not interfere with the scenes of Hotspur; he thanked me and refused it, saying he must have it performed according to his advertisement or not at all, for he must keep his word with the town; and so dismissed the house. This occasioned a pleasant scene, for immediately a terrible row ensued between the few who paid ready money and those who brought in his benefit tickets. The doorkeepers not being able to distinguish the real proprietors of the cash, would not refund a penny to either party. After some cuffs and blows the doors were shut in a great hurry, and all parties dispersed with great dissatisfaction."

The most important news Barry has to communicate is that he has had proposals made him on behalf of one of the London managers, "proposals vastly higher than my merit is

entitled to ; a hundred pounds in hand by way
of present, to engage me for one or more
seasons as I shall think proper—nay, every
reasonable advantage I can ask."

Barry, whom Garrick on his return to
London had spoken of as the best lover he
had ever seen on the stage, was eventually
engaged for Drury Lane. Miss Bellamy states
that he went away without giving the manager
any previous notice or paying any respect to
his articles. Though his loss must have been
felt, Sheridan was himself a force that could
not fail to draw. Summoning all his energy,
he began the winter of 1746 by opening a
subscription for six of Shakespeare's plays.
The first of these he performed was Much Ado
About Nothing, which was in no way successful. When The Merchant of Venice was
played, Miss Bellamy, as Portia, attracted some
attention by imitating Lord Chief Baron Bowes,
an infringement of good taste looked upon
with leniency at this period. Indeed, his
lordship, who witnessed her performance,
was so much pleased with her imitation that he
paid her many compliments upon the occasion.

Romeo and Juliet was the most successful play the manager staged that season ; for though Sheridan never had much of the lover in his composition, as Hitchcock says, " and was totally unfit to represent the tender sighing Romeo," yet Miss Bellamy's picturesque appearance and tender manner, together with the spectacle of a funeral procession, attracted the town, and the tragedy was given for nine nights to full houses, which was considered " an extraordinary circumstance at that time."

When by-and-by Dryden's tragedy of All for Love, or the World Well Lost, was pro-duced, it afforded extraordinary entertainment, in more senses than one. Sheridan had resolved to stage the play with great elegance, and having, during an excursion he had made to London in the summer, bought a superb suit of clothes of silver tissue which had been worn only on one occasion by the Princess of Wales, he elected that Miss Bellamy should appear in this, in her character of Cleopatra.

Accordingly this silver tissue suit was handed to the stage mantua maker to alter to Miss Bellamy's shape. The actress's maid, one Nancy

O'Brian, lent her services to the operation, and likewise sewed on the gown a number of diamonds lent for the occasion by Mrs. Butler. Their work being done, they hung the costume in the dressing-room and carelessly left the door ajar.

Now as luck would have it, who passed the way but Mrs. Furnival, who dially hated the young minx that greatly surpassed her in popularity, and against whom she had a special grudge since she had taken from her the character of Constance in King John. And seeing this gorgeous gown, Mrs. Furnival envied, and then resolved to appropriate it to her own use ; silver tissue sparkling with diamonds being far finer than her own costume of black velvet with tarnished gold braid. In an instant she wrapped up the costume and carried it to her room ; but scarce had she done so when careless Nancy O'Brian returned to discover it had disappeared.

On this she raised a terrible cry, running here and there in search of the missing garment and the jewels, her fright and agitation being beyond expression. Eventually she heard Mrs.

Furnival had got possession of the silver tissue, and to her the wrathful Nancy hastened, demanding the property in no very civil terms. Mrs. Furnival refused her request, whereon the blood of the kings of Ulster boiled in Nancy's veins, and without more ado she fell tooth and nail upon the actress, and with such violence that if assistance had not come to the screaming woman thus assaulted, it was certain her retirement for a time from the stage would have been inevitable.

The result was that Nancy was put out of the room, whilst her enemy retained possession of the gown. The maid now gave way to hysterical tears, and was found in this condition by her mistress, who hearing of the occurrence could not help feeling highly amused. She sent for the jewels and received word she should have them after the play.

There was nothing to be done but to don a gown of simple white satin, dressed in which she went to the green room, where the manager expressed his surprise and disappointment at her appearance. Refraining from telling him what had happened, she made an equivocal answer, and as it was time for him to appear on the stage no more was said. Light however was thrown on the subject when in a few moments Mrs. Furnival, as Octavia, made her resplendent appearance. Sheridan stared at her as he might at an apparition, and was so confused that he could not continue his part ; whilst at the same time Mrs. Butler, leaning from her box, interrupted the strange silence that fell upon the house by loudly exclaiming, "Good heavens, that woman has got on my diamonds."

Those who heard her immediately concluded she had been robbed of her jewels by Mrs. Furnival. The greatest consternation ensued; but seeing Sheridan smile, the audience concluded there was some joke connected with the affair, and so remained quiet until the act ended. By that time a whisper of the real cause of Mrs. Furnival's splendour had spread through the house, when a great cry went up, "No more Furnival. No more Furnival." On this the actress promptly called hysterical fits to her aid and her place was taken by another player. With such comic interruptions the performance of the tragedy could scarcely be called a success.

Though the theatre improved in many ways under Sheridan's management, there was one abuse which custom had so deeply rooted, that its eradication seemed difficult, if not impossible. This was the free admission of young bloods and college boys to the stage and behind the scenes. Any change in a fashion so long tolerated, it was feared, would excite the wrath and vengeance of a class whose power over the theatre was a force with which managers had to reckon. Seeing the inconvenience and abuse to which it led, Victor frequently had proposed measures for its remedy, when Sheridan invariably made reply, "You forget yourself; you think you are on English ground."

The remedy came in a manner and at a time least expected.

It happened on the evening of the 19th of January, 1747, whilst Sir John Vanburgh's comedy of Æsop was being played to a thin house, that a young blood named Kelly, from Galway, an unpolished fellow who was inflamed with wine, left his seat in the pit whilst the curtain was down, and climbing over the spikes with which it was thought necessary to protect the stage, made his way to the green room. Here he found the women who were taking part in the piece, and in drunken hilarity he set himself to address one of them, Mrs. Dwyer. But so grossly indecent were his words, that all of them took to flight, he pursuing Miss Bellamy, who sought refuge in her room. He then stationed himself outside her locked door, where he made such a noise as not only disturbed the performance then taking place on the stage, but frightened the young actress from answering her call and appearing on the boards.

At this point Sheridan came and commanded his servants to conduct Kelly " to the pit from whence he came." This the aggressor considered a mighty insult, and when Sheridan appeared upon the stage, Kelly took a basket from one of the orange women and pelted him with her wares. One of the oranges taking aim, Sheridan appealed to the public for protection, when some of those in the pit brought the roistering fellow to order; not however before he had called the manager a rascal and a scoundrelly player. To that Sheridan answered, " I am as good a gentleman as you are."

205

The play no sooner ended than Kelly, forcing his way by the stage entrance, rushed to Sheridan's room, where he repeated his abusive names, the result being that he was soundly thrashed by Sheridan, and took his drubbing with patience. But no sooner was he free to depart than he hied himself to Lucas's coffee-house, and exhibiting his bleeding nose and torn clothes, told his comrades that Sheridan's servants held him fast whilst their master beat him. To stir their wrath more deeply, he added that the manager had publicly declared himself as good a gentleman as any in the house.

Great was the consternation, greater the anger of the bucks and bloods at this astounding news. That a scoundrel of a player should dare to beat a gentleman, was an insult not to be borne. Vengeance must follow, full and soon. A powerful fighting party was formed, and all persons were openly threatened in the coffee-houses next day who dared to express themselves in Sheridan's favour.

It was not until some evenings later that the manager's name appeared on the bills, when he was announced to play Horatio in the Fair

Penitent. That day he received numerous anonymous letters and messages from friends warning him not to leave his house and begging him to have it well guarded. Acting on such advice he remained at home, happily for his security; for no sooner did one of the players come forward to apologize for Sheridan's absence, than some fifty young bucks, armed with swords and having Kelly at their head, rose with a shout, and climbing over the stage, rushed to the green room, where failing to find Sheridan, they searched the dressing-rooms, broke open all locked doors, and thrust their swords into wardrobes and chests of clothes by way of feeling for him, as they explained. As he was not discovered, they hurried in a body to his house, but finding it guarded, they discreetly avoided a fight.

Next day nothing was talked of but the attempt made upon Sheridan; coffee-houses rang with it; wine taverns were full of it, whilst it was the general topic of those who met in the streets. Expressions of sympathy for Sheridan were followed by violent threats, sometimes by sturdy blows. Presently letters appeared in the papers denouncing or applauding the conduct of the rioters, pamphlets followed, meetings were held, and the whole city, nay the whole kingdom, as Victor asserts, "was engaged in the quarrel, which not only threatened ruin to all whose bread was depending on the theatre, but the lives and fortunes of many without doors, who were so rash as to engage publicly in the affair, which was nothing more than the honour of an actor."

Strange to say the authorities did not interfere, but the public, seeing the injustice and brutality of the persecutors, resolved to support and defend the manager. They were probably strengthened in this determination by the knowledge that the College Boys, who had been out of town during the first stage of the quarrel, had now returned, and would side with Sheridan.

He was therefore advised to open the theatre, and to appear on its stage, where protection was guaranteed him. When therefore he was announced to play Richard III., the bloods were astounded at his impudence, and they loudly declared he would never be permitted to act until he had made submission and apologies to them.

On the night in question the doors were hardly opened when the house was filled; a vast number of women of quality and men of parts gave the support of their presence; the pit was thronged by undergraduates, who distributed themselves amongst the citizens, and in the boxes were Kelly's partisans. Intense excitement filled the atmosphere, expectation of a feud brightened the college boys; the gods were prepared to rain down vengeance in the shape of stones and bottles on Sheridan's enemies.

Now when these took their places in the boxes, a glance at the pit enabled them to see that it was thronged by undergraduates, who though sitting apart to conceal their numbers, were ready at a given signal to unite their strength. Knowing therefore what they might expect, the rioters kept quiet, and it was only at the end of the first act that some of them cried out, " Submission, apology ; off, off." Sheridan bowed respectfully and began to speak, but his words could not be heard because of the violent opposition which arose, and the answering cries of " No submission, no apology; go on with the play."

The noise was only silenced when Charles Lucas, a well-known politician and respected citizen, stood up in the pit and waved his hands to entreat silence. And this being granted, he said he presumed every sober citizen came to receive the entertainment promised in the bill and paid for at the door. The actors there were servants of the audience, and under their protection during the performance ; and he looked upon every insult or interruption given to them in the discharge of their duty, as offered to the audience. He moved that those who were for preserving the decency and freedom of the stage should hold up their hands. Shouts of applause greeted his words, and nearly the whole audience lifted their hands as he finished

Now at this point one of Kelly's friends, more indiscreet than his fellows, leaned out of his box and blew through a cat call, whereon one John Trot, who was under him in the pit, rose up and knocked him down. The wild cheers of delight that approved this action showed the Kellyites the danger of further interference just then, when they quietly left the house to mature their plans of vengeance.

One of these was soon after put into execution, when Charles Lucas was set upon and beaten by these fine gentlemen late at night. Next day he published an advertisement stating that a number of rude, disorderly persons in the habits of gentlemen, who for some time past had infested public places and disturbed the peace of the theatre, had recently assaulted a citizen, who now offered five pounds reward for the apprehension and conviction of any one of the offenders. This made them threaten fresh vengeance on him, hearing which he went armed with pistols, and enjoyed peace thereafter.

The time now arrived when a play was annually performed for the benefit of the Hospital for Incurables. The theatre was closed, but the Governors of the Hospital requested the manager to give him their benefit as usual, promising him their protection for the night. To this Sheridan consented, and the Fair Penitent was announced for performance. It was thought that an entertainment given for charity and sure to be witnessed by a number of ladies of quality, would not be disturbed. The College Boys, therefore, saw no necessity for their presence at the theatre that evening.

Long before the curtain rose a brilliant audience had assembled. The patronesses of the charity, radiant in beauty, with feather-bedecked heads and busts brilliant with jewels, occupied the boxes; a number of the most esteemed citizens thronged the pit, the two first benches of which were filled by Kelly's friends. This was noted with dismay, but it was hoped they would conduct themselves. When the curtain drew up over a hundred ladies were found seated on the stage, whose presence there was warmly greeted by the gallery. Then entered Sheridan, who was ushered in by the Governors of the Hospital, white wands in their hands, their faces full of satisfaction.

Scarce, however, had he made his appearance when the Kellyites, fully armed, rose to a man and boisterously ordered him off the stage. Sheridan immediately withdrew, when a violent dispute arose between these fine gentlemen and the Governors, threats were exchanged, and the violence increasing, challenges followed. Now amongst the Governors there was an under-graduate in his gown, who whilst warmly resenting this interference, was struck with an apple, and called a scoundrel.

Wild with rage at this indignity, he flew "like a feathered Mercury" to the college, and summoning all the boys within its walls at the time, told them of his treatment. Nothing could exceed their fury. Vowing vengeance, they tore through the streets, to find the theatre emptied of the rioters, who foreseeing their danger had hurried from the house. The students, however, were determined to punish those who had insulted one of their body, and in this resolve they were backed by some of the principals. Accordingly away they hied to search the coffee-houses and taverns where it was possible the offenders were, but not one of them was found. Their disappointment but increased their wrath. Returning to the University, they held a council of war which lasted through the night, when various plans for punishment were discussed.

And no sooner were the gates opened in the morning than out they sallied, excited, vociferous, eager for the fray. Various detachments were appointed to search houses and inns for the offenders, but especially for the individual who had flung the apple, to whom no mercy would be shown.

News of this uprising struck terror into the hearts of the Kellyites; some of them hid, others hurried in fear and trembling to the Court of Chancery, where they claimed protection. The citizens fearing a civil war, closed their shops, the watch made themselves invisible, a crowd of cheering, mischief-loving idlers followed the College Boys to assist their efforts if necessary, and at any rate to join in the fun.

It was not until eleven o'clock that the chief offender was found, when trembling amidst a howling crowd of hundreds he was hurried to the University and there secured. But before the undergraduates could satisfy themselves at least one other person must be discovered. This was a youth who had aided and abetted the apple thrower. He was known to be an officer who lived in Capel Street with his father, "a gentleman of three thousand a year." To his house the students went in the might of their numbers and demanded of its owner that he should deliver up his son. This being refused, they vowed to drag out the offender, and attempted to break into the mansion, which, however, was stoutly defended by servants. A free fight ensued, that ended by the boys effecting a breach and securing the object of their search. With victorious shouts they hurried him into a hackney coach, beside which they ran yelling with delight until they reached the college.

The Principals now interfered lest too violent measures should be taken ; however, the chief offender was made to go down on his bare knees in all the courts of the college and read aloud an abject apology prepared for him. His abettor, because of his holding the king's commission, was graciously permitted to read the same whilst standing, and both were then dismissed. By order of the Lords Justices, the Master of Revels now commanded the theatre, which had become a place of public disturbance, to be closed. Kelly and some of his friends were soon after prosecuted for assaulting Sheridan and injuring his property, whereon Kelly

took an action against the manager for assault
and battery. Before the trial Sheridan
published a defence pitiful to read, in which he
stated that all he required was the privilege
which every British subject had a right to
expect, that so long as he did not insult anyone
he should not be insulted. Having dwelt on
his endeavours to benefit the stage and referred to the recent riot, he adds he is willing
" that everything that regards himself be waived ;
and if those gentlemen will meet him and give
proper assurance to the town that they will
not disturb the entertainments for the future,
he will drop all prosecution against them, and
sit down content with his loss, which is already
so considerable as to destroy all hopes of profit
for this season."

This offer being declined with some show of
insolence, the law was permitted to take its
course. Nothing was talked of by all classes
but the approaching trial. The Kellyites felt
assured that success would attend their suit ;
their opponent was not certain of obtaining
justice. Report stated that hundreds were

being subscribed for the defence of these wanton and dissolute fellows ; it was believed the honesty of the jury would be tested.

" I was laughed to scorn," says Victor, "for believing a jury could be found in Dublin that would find a gentleman guilty. But when the time drew near the Lord Chief Justice Marlay sent for the High Sheriff and directed him to make out and bring a list of sufficient and able persons to his lordship. This message was immediately spread through the city, and as the usual iniquitous practices of under-sheriffs and packed jurors were intended for this case, the disappointment struck such a panic in the whole party that they gave themselves up as undone from that circumstance."

At last the day came when the suit was tried. The greatest legal lights of the land were employed on either side. From early in the morning the doors of the court were besieged by an interested and excited mob, which if it did not gain admission, could at least divert itself by seeing the principals and witnesses enter and depart. Mr. Justice Ward was appointed to hear both cases, but the Lord Chief Justice and a full Bench were likewise present, together with a vast number of men of quality and learning.

Sheridan was first put upon his trial for beating a gentleman; but so clear was the evidence regarding the provocation he had received, that the jury acquitted him without leaving the box. This was a triumph, but greater was to follow. A vast number of witnesses was summoned to prove Kelly's offence, and the trial was going steadily against him when Sheridan was called. The opposing counsel threw back his pugnacious head, thrust his thumbs under his armpits, and squaring himself, told the Court he was anxious to see a curiosity. "I have often seen," said this bravado, "a gentleman soldier, a gentleman sailor, but never have I laid eyes on a gentleman player."

"Then, sir," replied Sheridan, as he gravely turned, "you see one now," at which the court burst into applause.

Eventually a verdict of guilty was given against Kelly, who to the amazement of the town and the joy of many, was ordered to pay a fine of five hundred pounds and sentenced to

three months imprisonment. Moreover when
the latter had been pronounced, the Lord Chief
Justice, addressing the court, said that in future
attention would be paid to the gentlemen who
resorted to the theatre ; and if any persons
orced their way behind the scenes, and were
afterwards apprehended and brought before that
court, they should be made to feel the uttermost severity of the law. And from that hour,
Victor narrates, " not even the first men of
quality in the kingdom ever asked or attempted
to get behind the scenes."

The rumour which credited Kelly's friends
with subscribing hundreds for his defence was
false, and he was left to bear his penalty unaided.
But scarce had he been a week in confinement
when he solicited Sheridan to intercede on his
behalf. This the manager willingly did, and
with such effect that not only the fine was
remitted, but he went bail to the Court of
King's Bench " for the enlargement of the young
gentleman."

Sentries were now appointed to guard the
stage door and deny admission to those who had
no business behind the scenes. Notwithstanding

Victor's statement just quoted, this was not an unnecessary precaution; for Miss Bellamy tells us that one night when a young officer who had " more wine in his head than humanity in his heart" was not permitted to enter, he out with his sword and in the twinkling of an eye stabbed the guard in the thigh, using such violence that the blade broke "and left a piece in the most dangerous part." Immediately there was a terrible commotion, women screamed, men swore, a crowd gathered, the watch was called, the hero of the sword was threatened by the mob, and the sentry was carried to a hospital amid wails and lamentations. Here his wounded leg was amputated, in consequence of which he was provided for for life by his assailant.

CHAPTER X.

THE remainder of the season was uneventful, and at its close Sheridan went to London and secured Henry Woodward, an actor of merit in comedy, and the Michels, who were considered the best dancers on the stage. Woodward, who received five hundred pounds for the winter season, was engaged not only as a comedian but as a harlequin, in which he had gained great repute, and according to his articles he was bound to get up two or three old pantomimes and one new one at a limited expense.

On the evening of September 28, 1747, he made his first appearance before a Dublin audience, playing Marplot, in which he gained much applause. In a letter written by Benjamin Victor to Garrick a few weeks later, the former says that Woodward was very well liked ; one of his characters, Flash, being "beyond all things of the kind ever seen."

In the same letter he mentions a subject which was then perplexing his manager.

" We shall be obliged to you," he writes, " if in your next letter you will inform us, who are the persons belonging to the Royal Family that claim the liberty of your theatre. I mean if any, and who, every play night ? We all know there are an appointed number when the King or any of the Royal Family goes to the house. The reason of this inquiry is to form some application to the Lord Lieutenant to redress the insupportable grievance this theatre labours under. You know it is an old custom here for government to pay 100*l*. a year for the Governor and his court, and as the theatre royal is now under new management, a list has been made out (I suppose at the Secretary's office) of ninety-two persons who claim a free seat in the theatre every night if they please to demand it."

In due time two old pantomimes were produced, but though well got up and enlivened with excellent dancing they failed to produce profit. Greater things were expected from the new pantomime brought out in February, 1748, for which the town was well prepared by advertisements and paragraphs ; but the first night there was not a hundred pounds in the house, and though the Fair Penitent was played in front of it the second night, twenty pounds were not taken at the doors ; the fact being that pantomimes were entertainments which seldom or never attracted Dublin audiences.

Sheridan and Miss Bellamy were from time to time seen in Shakesperian performances, though the latter had little satisfaction in "playing with one so disqualified by nature" for romantic parts. In representing Cleopatra she sadly missed the "silver toned voice and bewitching figure of Barry who used to enchant the audience"; these qualities being succeeded by formality and monotonous declamation. Once, when the tragedy of Antony and Cleopatra was staged, a dance of gladiators was introduced, and likewise another effect which had not been rehearsed. This was on the entrance of one of the queen's attendants, to whose ragged tail a kettle-drum had attached itself. Alarmed at this uncommon noise, Cleopatra turned round, and seeing its cause burst out laughing, in which she was heartily joined by the house. " Nor could I compose my countenance," says Miss Bellamy, " till the asp had finished my night's duty."

Meanwhile the town was vastly diverted by a performer whose acquaintance it had made some years before. The *Dublin Journal* of March 5th, 1748, announced, "Mr. Foote is arrived from London to give Chocolate at 11 in the morning." Since his previous visit to Dublin Foote had fortunately discovered that the real bent of his genius lay in satire and mimicry, and to those qualities he gave full play, much to the diversion of the town. It was early in 1747 that he conceived the excellent idea of writing a play to suit the peculiarities of his talents, and of becoming his own manager. With characteristic daring he therefore hired the Haymarket Theatre, where, as no patent had been granted it, plays could not legally be performed. To meet the difficulty arising from the circumstance, he inserted the following advertisement on the 22nd of April :—

" At the Theatre in the Haymarket this day will be performed a Concert of Music, with which will be given *gratis* a new entertainment called *The Diversions of the Morning*, to which will be added a farce taken from the *Old Bachelor*, called *The Credulous Husband*— Fondlewife by Mr. Foote : with an Epilogue to be spoken by the Bedford Coffee House. To begin at 7."

A prodigious crowd awaited the opening of the doors. Great fun was expected, but more was enjoyed. The world affords no higher satisfaction than that of witnessing the follies and vanities, the assumptions and oddities, which beset our neighbours and friends—and are happily confined to them—ridiculed and burlesqued. The house roared and applauded as the mimic grew bolder and more personal ; but the greatest diversion of all arose from the fact that well-known players such as Garrick, Quin, Woffington, Ryan, and Mrs. Cibber were imitated with such whimsical absurdity, yet with such likeness to life, that there was no withstanding the humour of the portrayal.

This of course was calculated to ruin their popularity and injure their business, so that the managers of the great theatres declared Foote had infringed the law by performing a farce in a house which had no patent, and called for the intervention of the authorities. Accordingly when a crowd would have gathered a second time at the Haymarket doors, they were dispersed by a posse of constables.

Foote became elated by opposition, and his ingenious mind found a loophole out of the difficulty. Next day appeared an advertisement stating that, " On Saturday morning, exactly at 12 o'clock, at the New Theatre in the Haymarket, Mr. Foote begs the favour of his friends to come and drink a dish of chocolate with him ; and it is hoped there will be a great deal of comedy and some joyous spirits. He will endeavour to make the morning as diverting as possible. Tickets for this entertainment to be had at George's Coffee House, Temple Bar, without which no person will be admitted. N.B.—Sir Dilbury Diddle will be there, and Lady Betty Frisk has absolutely promised."

In this notice the town saw assurance of amusement, and accordingly high and low flocked to see the fun. And mirthful indeed was the performance when Foote came forward with a little band of players whom he made rehearse scenes from various favourite comedies and tragedies, he taking opportunity to mimic in the most absurd manner the actors and actresses who had made such parts their own. Nor were personages spared his ridicule who had made themselves notable by their foppery, egotism, dulness or pretence : whilst arrows of wit steeped in gall were aimed at the follies and fashions of the town. He soon became the rage, and women of quality and men of distinction filled the boxes of his theatre, though some smarted from his satire and others quailed on seeing themselves daringly mimicked to their faces.

His success in London was not repeated in Dublin, chiefly owing to the fact that the characters he ridiculed were not well-known in the Irish capital : and it was not until some seasons later that Foote undertook to oblige the town by boldly caricaturing the oddities that amused and the bores that plagued the people of Dublin.

Whilst Foote was performing at Capel Street, Sheridan, leaving Benjamin Victor to look after the affairs of the theatre, betook himself to London once more, there to engage fresh talent for the coming winter. Full of great enterprise and elated by hopes that experience had not checked, he resolved to secure the services of the best, regardless of outlay. As musical pieces were coming into fashion, he hired Mr. Lampe, then esteemed one of the best composers of the day, Signor Pasquali, a fine performer on the violin, Mrs. Mozeen, Mrs. Storer, Mrs. Lampe, Howard, and Sullivan, all mighty fine singers; their united salaries amounting to fourteen hundred pounds a season, at that time considered an extraordinary high figure to pay.

And as if these were not enough, he likewise engaged Mrs. Bland, a young actor named Storer, and Mr. and Mrs. Macklin, the last named couple being articled for two years at the amazing salary of eight hundred a year. Sheridan had by this time lost the services of Miss Bellamy, who becoming tired of the Irish stage, had refused to remain longer in the country, when going to England in the summer, she was engaged for Covent Garden Theatre.

Charles Macklin was an Irishman whose real name was M'Laughlin, a family that claimed descent from the old ancient kings of Ireland themselves. He had come into this world in evil times, for scarce was he two months old when the Battle of the Boyne was fought. Six of his uncles took creditable part in the siege of Derry, three within and three without the walls, from which it will be seen they were on different sides.

Full soon his father died and his mother married again, which probably did not tend to the boy's happiness ; neither did the fact that he was bound as apprentice to a saddler, who though a man of good repute for respectability in his calling, failed to understand the lad. At all events the latter made up his mind secretly to leave his employer and to seek his fortune in Dublin, he being then about the age of fourteen

years. Regarding the manner in which the
early months of his life in the capital were spent,
he ever after remained silent. Eventually he
became a badge man in Trinity College, where
he gained favour by his intelligence, and not
only received his stipulated allowance, but
additional aid from the students and fellows.

From Dublin he journeyed to England, where
he became a strolling player, and after some
years in the provinces presented himself, in 1725,
to Rich, the manager of Lincoln's Inn Fields
Theatre, who engaged him for a season, at the
end of which he was dismissed, " he telling me,"
says Macklin, " I spoke so familiar and so little
in the hoity-toity tone of the tragedy of that day,
that I had better go to grass for another year
or two."

Again he went strolling, this time into Wales,
and though here he endured drudgery and hard-
ship, in after years, when memory had softened
the slights and victory had crowned his endeavours, he was wont to say his experiences
were not the most unhappy of his life. When
sight of him is next obtained in London, on the
18th of September, 1730, he was playing Sir

Charles Freeman in the Beaux Stratagem, at Lee and Harper's great booth in the Bowling Green, Southwark. In the winter of that year he was again at Lincoln's Inn Fields, where in Fielding's comedy of The Coffee House Politician, he took the part of Porer in the first, and of Captain Brazencourt in the fifth act, when he received the first marks of applause. Again he went into the country, to return three years later, when he played Captain Brazen in The Recruiting Officer, at Drury Lane. It was at this theatre, then under the management of Fleetwood, that on the 23rd of September, 1734, Macklin appeared as Poins in Henry IV., from which time his estimation with the public gradually began to rise.

This, however, received a check not many months after he had sprung into note. Though like most men physically robust, he possessed high spirits, he had likewise a violent temper and an abusive tongue. Now it happened on the evening of May 10th, 1735, when he and another actor named Hallam were preparing to play in a new farce called Trick for Trick, the latter got possession of a wig which was the

231

property of the house, but which, having worn the preceding evening, Macklin now claimed as his right to wear. This Hallam refused, whereon much foul language was used on both sides, until at length Macklin becoming incensed, made a sudden lunge of his stick at Hallam, which struck the latter in the eye, penetrated his brain, and caused his death.

To avoid the consequences Macklin disappeared, but seven months later, on the 12th of December, he surrendered himself at the Old Bailey, where he was tried and found guilty of manslaughter. Apparently he suffered no punishment, for on the 31st of the following month he was playing the part of Ramillie in Fielding's Miser. This accident was unsuccessful in teaching him to control his temper, for three years later he fell foul of Quin, and though their quarrel was subsequently made up, the bitterness of its remembrance remained with them through life.

The quarrel itself was brought about in this way. During the run of Wycherley's Plain Dealer, the actor who played Jerry Blackacre was taken suddenly ill, on which Macklin represented the character, which he dressed in red breeches. Quin ridiculed this taste, which Macklin defended warmly; abuse followed, that ended abruptly by Quin throwing an orange in Macklin's face. The latter closed with the offender, a scuffle took place, when Macklin pommelled him damnably. As a consequence Quin remained in retirement for several days, whilst Macklin played his parts as usual. After this they avoided each other's company, and when they met at rehearsals were coldly civil. The manner in which some show of friendship was established is strikingly characteristic of the times.

On the evening of a day when both had attended a fellow-player to his last home, they found themselves, with others, at a tavern in Covent Garden. As the night passed, their companions gradually dropped off until the antagonists were face to face and alone. After some minutes of silence, during which they seemed surprised at their situation, Quin drank Macklin's health, and this the latter courteously returned. The pause which then followed was more awkward yet, when Quin resolving to end it began,

" There has been a foolish quarrel between you and me, sir, which though accommodated, I must confess I have not been able to forget till now. The melancholy occasion of our meeting, and the circumstances of our being together, I thank God, have made me see my error. If therefore you can forget it, give me your hand, and let us live together in future like brother per-formers."

Macklin instantly gave his hand, a fresh bottle was called for and others followed, when eventually, in the grey light of morning, Macklin, being unable to find a chair to convey his drunken companion, carried him home on his back.

The greatest success of Macklin's career was made by his representation of Shylock. So far back as 1701, Lord Lansdowne had produced a comedy entitled The Jew of Venice, in which he had taken the liberty of altering Shakespeare's play and making Shylock a comic character. And as such it had continued to be played until February 14th, 1741, when Macklin, gaining a reluctant consent from his manager, produced the play as originally

written, and acted Shylock with such force,
colour, and truth to nature, that he took the
town by storm, and won a high place in his
profession. "On my return to the green-room,"
Macklin afterwards said, in speaking of that
memorable night, "it was crowded with nobility
and critics who all complimented me in the
warmest and most unbounded manner, and the
situation I found myself in, I must confess, was
one of the most flattering and intoxicating of
my whole life. No money, no title, could purchase what I felt. And let no man tell me after
this, what fame will not inspire a man to do, and
how far the attainment of it will not remunerate
his greatest labours. Though I was not worth
fifty pounds in the world at that time, yet let
me tell you I was Charles the Great for that
night."

As a player of distinction, he was now
invited to the tables of the nobility, and it
happened that one day being bidden by Lord
Bolingbroke to dine with him at Battersea, the
actor there met Alexander Pope the poet, who
questioned him about his conception of Shylock,
and asked him why he wore a red hat. Mack-

lin replied that he had read the Jews in Italy, especially in Venice, wore hats of that colour. "And pray, Mr. Macklin," asked the poet, "do players in general take such pains?"

" I do not know, sir, that they do," answered Macklin ; "but as I had staked my reputation on the character, I was determined to spare no trouble in getting at the best information."

"Very laudable indeed," assented Pope, as he tapped his snuff-box, "very laudable indeed." On which the player bowed, feeling highly honoured by the compliment.

Quin, who played Antonio to Macklin's Shylock, was not so complimentary. When on the first night Macklin walked into the green-room ready dressed for Shylock, his appearance caused much attention, which was not without an element of amusement.

" Now," said Quin, turning to Milward, who was the Bassanio of the cast, "if God Almighty writes a legible hand, that man must be a villain."

"He has strong lines on his face which are always serviceable to an actor," replied Milward.

"Lines?" repeated Quin, in astonishment, "I see nothing in the fellow's face but a damn deal of cordage."

Mrs. Macklin, who had been the widow of a Dublin hosier before becoming the wife of an irascible player, was an excellent actress. As the nurse in Romeo and Juliet, and as the Hostess in King Henry V., she was admirable, whilst her representations of fine ladies and winsome widows in the comedies of the day, were pronounced unequalled in their merit.

The Dublin season opened with every promise of success, Charles Macklin playing such favourite characters of his as Shylock; Ben, in Love for Love; Sir Gilbert Wrangle in The Refusal; whilst his wife represented the nurse in Romeo and Juliet; Lady Wrangle, Lady Wronghead, and a variety of comedy characters which were greatly admired.

When winter came, an allegorical piece or dramatic opera called Jack the Giant Queller, written by Henry Brooke, the author of Gustavus Vasa, was produced at great expense. This opera which was in five acts, had no less than fifty-one songs, many of them written with great ingenuity and with a satire which manager and author alike considered could give no offence to those of honest and upright principles. However, as two or three ditties referred to Governors, Lord Mayors, and Aldermen in slighting terms, " some weak person belonging to the Government," who was present on the evening of its first production, went off to the Lords Justices and made complaints against the piece, whereon the Master of the Revels, without deigning to make inquiries, immediately forbade its performance ; and so what promised to prove profitable was not seen a second time that season.

Nor was this the sole trouble that beset Sheridan, for scarcely had Macklin been a month in Dublin, when his unconciliatory manner, suspicious disposition, and intolerable temper, began to make themselves disagreeably felt.

And no sooner had the novelty of his acting begun to wane, than Sheridan saw it was necessary to alternate the comedies in which Macklin played, with the tragedies in which the manager himself excelled. This was highly displeasing to Macklin, especially when the tragedies attracted greater houses than the comedies. He would then strut about the green-room swearing that Sheridan was "manager mad," and would seek to entertain audiences at wine taverns with disquisitions on his own marketable fame.

To those around he became gruff and irritable, and the quality of his temper may be gauged from an occurrence that took place on the stage. His acting was distinguished by three pauses, each longer than the other, according to the dignified impression he sought to convey, the last being styled his grand pause. One night when he had arrived at this point of his performance, the prompter imagined he had forgotten his words, and accordingly whispered them. As no notice was taken of this, he again and in a louder tone suggested the words, when Macklin rushed across the stage and knocked him down ; then returning, he told the audience " the fellow interrupted me in my grand pause," and continued his part.

His jealousy of Sheridan increasing, he swore that he would not tolerate the appearance on the bills of the manager's name in letters that were larger even by a hair's-breadth than his own ; and it was comical to see him produce a pair of compasses to measure the type in which their respective names were printed. Moreover when he had drunk too much claret, which was not infrequent, he became shamefully abusive.

However, Sheridan patiently bore with Macklin's temper for the first season, but eventually it became unendurable. The elder actor's aggressiveness reached an intolerable pitch when one night at the close of the performance he went out and announced a play for his wife's benefit without deigning to consult the manager regarding the piece or the date of its production. High words followed this breach of discipline, and Sheridan gave orders that this troublesome player was not to be admitted into the theatre from that time forward. Macklin sought redress from the law, and filed a bill in Chancery against his manager, when the latter paid three hundred pounds into court ; a sum which Macklin took rather than remain unemployed in Dublin whilst awaiting the slow progress of his suit.

Whilst in Dublin it was his delight to occupy a prominent place in some coffee house, where those who loved fun gathered round him to inflate his vanity and provoke his ire against those whom he imagined had offended him. On one occasion he overheard a man sitting at a neighbouring table laud Sheridan, when looking closely at the speaker he recognized him as a member of the Smock Alley band. On this Macklin shouted to him, " I believe, sir, you are a trumpeter ? "

" Well, sir, what if I am ? " the other asked in surprise.

" Nothing more, sir, than that being a trumpeter you are a dealer in puffs."

When he wished to be especially entertaining it was his custom to snatch off his wig and throw it to one side ; then as if relieved he would launch out into praise of his own achievements, and give specimens of his wit. It was when he was wigless one day that an Irish Church dignitary not remarkable for his veracity was complaining that he had been called a liar by a tradesman in his parish. Macklin inquired what reply he had made.

" I told him a lie was amongst the sins I dare
not commit," answered the parson.

" And why, sir," inquired Macklin, "did you
give the rascal so mean an opinion of your
courage ? "

At the close of the season that had introduced
"the musical tribe," Sheridan realized that he
had made a woeful bargain, for the profits of their
entertainments did not exceed a hundred and
fifty pounds, the sum paid for writing the scores
of their performances. As they were articled
for another season, Victor contrived to transfer
them to a musical society that gave entertainments in Fishamble Street, which was a happy
release to the manager.

Still keeping a brave heart, Sheridan sought
fresh attraction for his audiences and engaged
Theophilus Cibber, West Digges, and Henry
Mossop. The first of these was already well
known to the town ; the second, from his social
position and the circumstances attending his
life, engaged the attention of the politest circles ;
whilst the third became the favourite of all
undergraduates.

West Digges, who at this time was in his

twenty-ninth year, was son of a colonel in the Guards, a man of family and fortune nearly allied to some of the first nobility. Speculations in the South Sea scheme entailed the loss of his family estates to Colonel Digges, and his misfortunes preying upon his mind, hastened his death. His eldest son West was left to the guardianship of the Duke of Montague and the Earl de la Warr, to whose title and estates he remained heir-presumptive until he reached the age of eighteen, at which time Lady de la Warr inconsiderately gave birth to a son.

West Digges was then given a commission in the army. Having been " bred with elevated views," he contracted extravagant habits that soon led him into debt. He therefore sold his commission and turned his attention to the stage, which held a thousand charms for his imagination. Knowing that the interest of his indignant family would prevent him from being engaged by the London managers, he acted on the advice of Theo. Cibber and offered his services to Sheridan, who promptly engaged him.

Nature had bestowed favours on him bountifully. His face was handsome and expressive, his figure tall and graceful, his manner winning, refined and polished. No man was a greater favourite with the fair sex, a more desired companion with his own. His first appearance was made on the 27th of November, 1749, when the tragedy of Venice Preserved was announced, Sheridan playing Pierre; Cibber, Renault; whilst Jaffier was personated by "Mr. Digges, a gentleman lately arrived from England, who never yet appeared on any stage."

The news that this "gentleman actor" and some time heir-presumptive to an earldom was to appear on the stage, created general curiosity, and long before the night arrived on which he was to make his bow to the public, the boxes and circles were bespoke by women of quality and men of parts, all anxious to see this phenomenon. Amidst the general bustle and excitement before and behind the stage, none was more cool than he who was its cause. Victor, who stood by him at his first entrance, observed that "not a single nerve seemed disordered." The audience saluted him with peals of applause, to which he bowed in a finished manner, and then went on with his part in an intrepid way; his elegant deportment, ease of gesture, and natural grace delighting all who beheld him, his one blemish being a certain harshness of voice, save for which he might have rivalled Barry himself.

The sensation he caused had not time to sub-side when another novice was announced to appear. This was Henry Mossop, likewise a gentleman player; his father being the Rector of Tuam. Henry had been educated in a Dublin grammar school, and later had taken his degrees in Trinity College. He then betook himself to London, where an uncle promised to provide for him, but his temper and ambition not proving harmonious to his relative, he left him and sought employment on the stage.

Rich, of Covent Garden, and Garrick, of Drury Lane, to whom he gave specimens of his ability, pronounced him to be totally unfitted for the boards; but these opinions not altering his own as to his qualifications, he applied to Sheridan, who gave him a hearty invitation to try his fortunes at Aungier Street.

He made his bow in the tragedy of The Revenge; "the part of Zanga by Mr. Mossop, a gentleman of this kingdom who never appeared on any stage." In one quality, and in that only, did he excel Digges; for Mossop's voice was strong, harmonious, and capable of infinite modulation. His actions were awkward and unpicturesque, his delivery mechanical, and from his frequent habit of placing one hand on his hip whilst he elevated the other, he was likened to a teapot. For all that, we are told that he "displayed an astonishing degree of beautiful wildness;" and at times "such extraordinary marks of genius broke forth, as evidently indicated his future greatness, and confirmed his friends and the audience in the sanguine expectations they had formed of his abilities."

His friends and the audience were synonymous terms; for the pit was crowded with undergraduates who true to their traditions, had come to support a fellow-student. A prosperous and brilliant season now set in, and rewarded the efforts of so excellent a company, so that at its close the receipts were found to exceed those of previous seasons by the substantial sum of two thousand pounds.

For the winter season, beginning in September, 1750, Sheridan engaged Miss Cole, "a pleasing little actress from Drury Lane"; Monsieur Billione and Madame Paget, two capital dancers brought from Paris; James Robertson and Thomas King. Robertson, "a native of Ireland and one of its esteemed ornaments," was the author of "The Universal History," from the profits of which he purchased an annuity for his wife, who died soon after. Later he wrote poems, novels, prologues, and epilogues, and eventually, being a man of many talents, he took to the stage, where this child of the muses gained distinction as a comedian.

Tom King, who was at this time barely twenty, had been born in London and educated at Westminster School. His prudent father bound him to the law, but the youth's errant fancy attracted him to the stage. So one fine day he ran away in company with another lad, and joined a travelling company of players at Tonbridge, where he recited a prologue and an epilogue, took two parts in Hamlet, and represented Sharp in The Lying Lover, all for the sum of fourpence. He acted in barns, he

strutted in booths, and in the hard and wholesome school of experience gained that knowledge of his art which stood him in good stead.
Eventually, whilst at Windsor, he was seen by
Garrick, who engaged him for Drury Lane,
where he acquitted himself so well in a variety
of characters that he was soon held in high
esteem. He made his first appearance under
Sheridan's management at Smock Alley
Theatre in September, 1750, as Ranger in The
Suspicious Husband, when he showed
abilities that soon gained him the applause of
Dublin audiences.

From such an array of talent the manager
expected profitable results; nor was he disappointed. His treasurer, Victor, in writing to
Sir William Wolseley in December, 1750, says
that " entertainments were never in so high a tide
of favour as now. We have the famous Turk
from London who exhibits at Aungier Street
Theatre on Tuesdays and Saturdays; and we
have four plays a week at Smock Alley
Theatre, from all of which I have received six
hundred pounds a week, for many weeks past—
great doings for Dublin."

Though Mossop and Digges continued favourites with the public, yet their novelty soon began to wear away; curiosity regarding them was satisfied. Success did not lessen Mossop's opinion of his abilities, nor sweeten his temper, so that it became difficult to maintain friendship with him. Once when he elected to play Richard and dressed the character in " white satin puckered," the manager ventured to remark that "it had a most coxcombly appearance," which was repeated to Mossop, who in a storm of passion sought Sheridan in his room, and addressing him, said in his emphatic manner, " Mr. She-ri-dan, I hear you said I dressed Richard like a cox-comb; that is an af-front. You wear a sword, pull it out of the scabbard; I'll draw mine and thrust it into your bo-dy." The poor manager could but smile at this bloodthirsty design set out in so deliberate a manner; explanations followed, and peace was proclaimed.

But a man of such a temperament could not be expected to live in harmony with his fellows. Before long he quarrelled with Sheridan, and in May, 1751, suddenly left him and set out for London, where he was engaged by Garrick.

It was in this month that Peg Woffington arrived in Dublin, though not engaged by Sheridan. A coolness had sprung up between herself and Garrick, now manager of Drury Lane. Arthur Murphy states he had heard Peg Woffington "at different times declare that she was so near being married to Garrick that he had tried the wedding-ring on her finger." David, however, wedded another woman, and Peg would act under his régime no more. She had then transferred her services to Rich, of Covent Garden, but eventually had disagreed with him, and therefore at the end of the summer season had crossed the Channel with the idea of appearing on the Dublin stage. Sheridan, however, had no desire to enlist her in his company, for as he had not seen her act for some years he was not inclined to rate her abilities higher than those of Mrs. Bland, who was then articled with him. Moreover, he was anxious to hire Italian singers and produce operas, and he could not afford to give great salaries to her and them.

Victor, who had heard of her recent wonderful success in London, persuaded Sheridan to engage her, which he eventually did at a salary of four hundred pounds for the season—and then succeeded a period of brilliancy in the theatre, and of excitement in the town, such as was long afterwards remembered.

END OF VOL. I.